"Take your hands off the lady, or you're dead."

From beside her, the stranger's low-timbered voice was calm, but laced with lethal intent. The hair on Elisabeth's neck stood up.

No one else was privy to the robber's predicament. The green-eyed man's gun was still concealed between the two men, the business end jammed up against the robber's belly. Elisabeth dared a glance and saw the stranger's other hand clamped over the man's wrist, keeping that revolver pointed toward the floor and protectively away from her.

What could only have been seconds, but seemed like an hour, passed with their ragged breaths loud and the tick of a pocket watch encroaching on her consciousness.

"We ain't got all day, Hank!" one of the other thieves shouted.

The robber leaning over her attempted to move, and pandemonium broke loose. A shot rang out and Elisabeth's rescuer grunted in pain. The robber tugged at Elisabeth's collar, and the man beside her fired his gun.

The stench of gunpowder stung her nose. Men shouted. Women screamed. Elisabeth watched the events unfold in a haze of fear and disbelief.

Books by Cheryl St.John

Love Inspired Historical

The Preacher's Wife
To Be a Mother
  "Mountain Rose"
Marrying the Preacher's Daughter

CHERYL ST.JOHN

A peacemaker, a romantic, an idealist and a discouraged perfectionist are the words that Cheryl uses
to describe herself. The award-winning author of
both historical and contemporary novels says she's
been told that she is painfully honest.

Cheryl admits to being an avid collector, displaying
everything from dolls to depression glass, as well
as white ironstone, teapots, cups and saucers, old
photographs and—most especially—books. When
not doing a home improvement project, she and her
husband love to browse antiques shops. In her spare
time, she's an amateur photographer and a pretty
good baker.

She says that knowing her stories bring hope and
pleasure to readers is one of the best parts of being a
writer. The other wonderful part is being able to set
her own schedule and have time to work around her
growing family.

Cheryl loves to hear from readers! Email her at
SaintJohn@aol.com.

CHERYL ST.JOHN

Marrying the Preacher's Daughter

Love Inspired

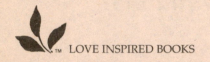 LOVE INSPIRED BOOKS

ISBN-13: 978-0-373-82872-2

MARRYING THE PREACHER'S DAUGHTER

Copyright © 2011 by Cheryl Ludwigs

www.LoveInspiredBooks.com

Printed in U.S.A.

And all these blessings shall come on thee, and overtake thee, if thou shalt hearken unto the voice of the Lord thy God. Blessed shalt thou be in the city, and blessed shalt thou be in the field. Blessed shall be the fruit of thy body, and the fruit of thy ground, and the fruit of thy cattle, the increase of thy kine, and the flocks of thy sheep. Blessed shall be thy basket and thy store. Blessed shalt thou be when thou comest in, and blessed shalt thou be when thou goest out.

—*Deuteronomy* 28:2–6

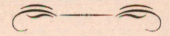

This story is lovingly dedicated to the readers who so patiently waited for Elisabeth's story. I appreciate you!

Chapter One

Colorado
June, 1876

"Toss your guns down now!" a male voice shouted. "Hands in the air."

Elisabeth Hart couldn't see past the layers of netting on a woman's hat in front of her, but sounds of alarm rippled through the passengers who sat in the forward rows. The interior of the railcar was sweltering beneath the midday sun, and she blotted her eyes and forehead with her lace-trimmed handkerchief. What should have been a routine stop along the tracks to take on water had become life-threatening.

Thuds sounded as firearms hit the aisle. A man in a battered hat and wearing a faded bandanna over the lower half of his face came into view. Eyes darting from person to person, he snatched up the guns.

Another masked bandit appeared in the wake of the first. Sweat drenched the front of his dusty shirt. "Turn over all your cash and jewelry. Ladies' bags, too, and none of you gets shot."

Two more thieves held open gunnysacks and gathered the looted items.

Fear prickled at Elisabeth, but a maelstrom of rebellious anger made her tremble. How dreadful of these men to point guns and make demands. Every fiber of her being objected to their lack of concern for the safety of the passengers and the downright thievery.

She turned to the tall, quiet man who'd been sitting beside her on the aisle side of the bench seat since they'd left Morning Creek, noting the way his hat brim shaded piercing green eyes. He watched the gunman with intense concentration, but made no move to stop what was happening. "Aren't you going to *do something?*" she whispered.

The man cast her a glare that would have scorched a lesser woman. One eyebrow rose and he gave an almost imperceptible shake of his head.

"They're going to rob us," she insisted. "You still have your gun. I saw it inside your jacket when you leaned to lower the window earlier."

He focused on the man wielding the revolver, but spoke to her. "Can you count, lady? Just give 'em what they want so nobody gets hurt."

"But—"

Pausing beside them, the masked robber pointed his gun directly at her seat partner's chest. The man gave Elisabeth a pointed glare and calmly raised his hands in the air before looking up.

"Right in here," the robber said.

The seated man handed him a coin purse and tossed several silver dollars and his pocket watch into the bag.

The barrel of the gun swung to Elisabeth. "Lady?"

Elisabeth's temper and sensibilities flared, but fear kept her silent. Her heart beat so frantically, she thought her chest might burst. She wanted to refuse, but didn't want anyone to get hurt. Begrudgingly, she forfeited her black velvet chatelaine pocket with the silver handle and removed the gold bracelet she'd received for her last birthday, dropping both into the burlap sack.

The robber pointed at her neck. "You got a chain under there."

She clapped her hand protectively over the plain gold ring that rested on a chain beneath her damp and wrinkled cotton shirtwaist. "This was my mother's!"

"Just give it to him," the green-eyed stranger cajoled in his maddeningly calm manner.

"Now just wait," Elisabeth argued with a glare. "You don't understand. This was my *mother's* wedding ring."

The stranger gave her a quelling look that singed her eyelashes. Passengers called out their displeasure and shouted for her to give up her jewelry same as they had.

The ring was all she had of her mother. Since she'd drowned, Elisabeth had worn it every day…and tried to fill the woman's shoes. The wedding band symbolized Elisabeth's childhood and her sacrifices. Parting with it would break her heart…but she didn't want to be the cause of anyone getting shot. What would her father have to say in this situation?

She closed her eyes. *Do not store up for yourselves treasures on earth, where moth and rust destroy, and where thieves break in and steal.* Her true treasures were in heaven. The ring wasn't as important as the lives at stake.

The robber leaned down close as if he meant to take the ring from her neck. She raised her hand to her throat to prevent him from touching her. She could do this on her own. He grabbed Elisabeth's collar and yanked so hard that she jerked forward and the top button popped off.

In that same second, a grim click sounded. The bandit paused dead still.

Elisabeth stared into his shining dark eyes, and the moment stretched into infinity. She could hear her blood pulsing through her veins, her breath panting from between her dry lips. Was this the day she was going to die and meet her Maker?

"Take your hands off the lady, or you're dead." From beside her, the stranger's low-timbered voice was calm, but laced with lethal intent. The hair on Elisabeth's neck stood up.

No one else was privy to the robber's predicament. The green-eyed man's gun was still concealed between the two men, the business end jammed up against the robber's belly. Elisabeth dared a glance and saw the stranger's other hand clamped over the man's wrist, keeping that revolver pointed toward the floor and protectively away from her.

What could only have been seconds, but seemed like an hour, passed with their ragged breaths loud and the tick of a pocket watch encroaching on her consciousness.

"We ain't got all day, Hank!" one of the other thieves shouted.

The robber leaning over her attempted to move, and pandemonium broke loose. A shot rang out and Elisabeth's rescuer grunted in pain. The robber tugged at Elisabeth's collar, and the man beside her fired his gun.

The stench of gunpowder stung her nose. Men shouted. Women screamed. Elisabeth watched the events unfold in a haze of fear and disbelief.

The man who'd threatened Elisabeth crumpled, slumping sideways over the back of a seat. A horrifying crimson blotch spread across his shirtfront. She covered her mouth with her hand to keep from crying out.

The stranger leaped from his seat with his arm outstretched. "Get down!" he bellowed. A rapid succession of shots nearly deafened her. She cupped her hands over her ears, belatedly realizing he'd been ordering *her* to get down. Praying for safety for the other passengers, she folded herself onto the floor and knelt with her heart pounding. The shock of seeing that man shot and bleeding stole her breath.

Minutes passed with her thoughts in chaos. Would she see her family again? If the stranger protecting her had been shot, maybe other people were being killed or injured, and all because she'd delayed. She'd been going to give him the ring.

An eerie silence followed in the wake of the previous pandemonium, and it took a few minutes to comprehend what that could mean.

The sound of hesitant footsteps and voices told her the battle was over. She opened eyes she hadn't realized were squeezed shut, unfolded her body and peered over the seat in front of her.

One of the male passengers had picked up the gunny-sacks and now doled possessions back to their owners. In numb silence, she accepted her monogrammed velvet pocket and gold bracelet from his outstretched hand while her mind struggled to comprehend what was going on around her. A conductor and several other railroad men stepped over prone bodies on the floor. The sight made her stomach lurch. Elisabeth could only stare in numb disbelief.

One of the uniformed men made his way to the stranger who was seated on a bench with his back against the side of the railcar, his hand pressed to his ribs. "Find something for bandages!"

Spurred out of her frozen state of shock, Elisabeth straightened and stepped into the aisle. She raised her hem and, holding it in her teeth, tore a wide strip from her petticoat. "Here."

Others provided handkerchiefs and scarves, and the conductor handed over the wad of material for the fellow to press against the wound. "Sit tight," he said. "We'll get you to the doctor in Jackson Springs quick as we can."

Several men dragged the robbers' bodies to the back of the car, the dead men's boot heels painting shiny streaks of blood on the wooden floor. Her stomach roiled and she thought she might be sick.

"Are you all right?"

She swung her gaze to those green eyes, now dark with pain. "Y-yes, I'm fine."

Had he killed all of those men? He made a half-hearted attempt to sit a little straighter, but grimaced and stayed where he was.

He'd probably saved her life. Without a doubt he'd saved her from losing her precious ring. She perched on the edge of the seat beside his leg, and reached to replace his hand with hers, pressing the cloth against his cream-colored shirt, where it was soaked with blood that flowed from his side. "I'm Elisabeth Hart."

"Gabe Taggart," he replied.

"That was a very brave thing you did."

His expression slid into a scowl. "Didn't have much choice after the stupid thing you did."

Taken aback, she was at a loss for words. Before that horrible man had reached for her, she'd been prepared to hand over the ring. Now she felt foolish for ever hesitating.

Steam hissed and the train jerked into motion, picking up speed along the tracks. The stranger winced at the jerking movement. The woman who'd been sitting behind them made her way along the aisle in the rocking car. "Thank you for rescuing us," she said to Gabe.

Casting a disapproving scowl at Elisabeth, she returned to her seat. Elisabeth glanced at a few of the other occupants of the railcar and noted an assortment of scathing looks directed toward her. None of them understood the value she placed on the ring or the reason for her delay. She hadn't meant to endanger anyone.

Silently, she prayed for his life, asking God to forgive her for putting him at risk because of her selfish attachment to an earthly treasure. Out of habit, she reached into the jacket pocket of her traveling suit and rubbed a smooth flat stone between her fingers. The keepsake was one of several she'd picked up during her family's perilous journey to Colorado. The stones reminded her of the sacrifice and dedication that had brought them to a new state and a new life.

The train rocked and turned a bend. Several other passengers expressed their thanks to Gabe as the train neared its destination. When at last they reached Jackson Springs, the tale spread to the baggage men and the families waiting on the platform. Several men carefully loaded Gabe Taggart into the bed of a wagon and drove him away.

Grateful this particular chapter of her life was over and that Taggart would be getting medical attention now, Elisabeth released a pent-up breath and joined the others disembarking.

"Thank the Lord, you're safe."

Elisabeth turned with relief and embraced her stepmother, their bodies separated by the girth of Josie's growing belly beneath her pretty green day dress.

"What happened to that man?" her six-year-old half brother Phillip asked. He had shiny black hair like their father's and a sprinkling of freckles across his nose and cheeks.

"He prevented robbers from stealing our things," Elisabeth answered, trying to keep panic and guilt from her voice.

"Lis-bet, Lis-bet!" Peter and John, the three-year-old twins, jumped up and down waiting for her to greet them.

She picked up Peter first, kissing his cheek and ruffling his curly reddish hair. After setting him down, she reached for John. He kissed her cheek, leaving a suspiciously peppermint stickiness on her skin.

Josie turned and motioned forward a slender dark-haired young woman that Elisabeth had assumed was waiting for another passenger. "This is Kalli Tyler. She's my new helper. Your father thought I needed someone full-time, and I didn't argue. She's a godsend, truly. You two are going to get along well."

"I've heard all about you," Kalli said with a friendly dimpled smile. "Are you sure you're all right?"

"Yes, I'm fine." She kept her voice steady, but her insides quivered in the aftermath of that drama. She collected herself to study the other young woman.

As her father's assistant, the notary public and a tutor, Elisabeth did have her hands full. It was wise of Father and Josie to hire additional help. At seventeen and sixteen, her sisters, Abigail and Anna, were busy with school, studies and social activities, and their bustling household did need extra assistance to keep things running smoothly.

"I brought a wagon and Gilbert," Josie told her. "You had bags, and I'm not up to the walk."

"Of course," Elisabeth answered. "Phillip, help me find my bags, please."

She turned toward the pile where luggage was being stacked just as two men carried one of the robbers from the train on a stretcher. He'd been shot in the chest and his vest was drenched with dark glistening blood. The man was quite plainly dead.

Chapter Two

"Stop!" Stunned, Elisabeth grabbed her little brother and spun him away from the sight. "We'd better wait until the crowd thins out so we can find my satchels." Thankfully, the throng of onlookers had prevented Phillip from seeing what she'd just witnessed.

"I wanna see!" He wriggled, but she held him fast, staying behind him and keeping him faced the other way.

Josie had to give him a stern look before he stopped struggling. Finally, he leaned back against Elisabeth. Regret ate at her stoic confidence. Her ring definitely didn't seem as important as it had before. Especially if her hesitation had been the cause of these men's deaths. She swallowed hard.

At last the final body was removed and the crowd thinned. Phillip joined her in locating her satchel and another bag and carried the biggest one with both hands on the handle, the weight of the case banging against his shins.

A tanned hand reached to take the leather bag from him, and Elisabeth glanced up. "Gil!"

Her longtime friend was now a deputy. The silver star on his vest winked in the sunlight. He wore his hat cocked back, revealing his smiling blue eyes, and his familiarity was a comfort. "Heard there was some excitement," he said.

He hefted both bags into the back of the wagon, and while her family climbed onto the seat and over rails into the wagon bed, she gave him a friendly hug.

"You're trembling, Lis."

"I'm a little shaken up, I guess."

He was the only person ever allowed to call her by a shortened version of her name. At about sixteen, she'd stopped letting his teasing bother her, and thereafter it had become his habit. "I'm glad you weren't involved."

"Well, actually..."

"Actually what?"

She thought better of what she'd been about to reveal and pulled away. "Actually, I read an entire book in the two evenings I was in Morning Creek," she answered, avoiding her involvement.

"You're a wild one, you are," he said and helped her up to the bed beside her younger siblings and Kalli. Josie was on the springed seat, and he climbed up beside her. "I'm going to deliver you home, but I need to get right back and help with the paperwork and identifying the—uh—criminals."

Kalli occupied the boys by singing a nursery rhyme, and Elisabeth was grateful for the distraction she provided. Gil halted the team at the bottom of the hill, where the church sat beside a tiny empty parsonage.

Her father exited the church's side door and crossed the lawn, his black hair shining in the afternoon sun and a smile on his handsome face.

"Papa, there was robbers on the train!" Phillip called.

Samuel Hart's smile faltered and he studied Elisabeth with concern. "Are you all right?"

She jumped down to embrace him, and gave him a brief explanation.

"I'll head over to Dr. Barnes's to pray for the wounded hero," her father said. Elisabeth had expected nothing less of her father, a man of compassion and faith.

Gil led the team up the hill toward their home at the top of the tree-lined street. When the shrubbery and mature trees that surrounded their vast yard came into view, Elisabeth sighed with appreciation. Josie had been a wealthy widow when Father had married her, and her inheritances had supplied this dwelling where, in the years since, love had abounded and faith flourished.

While the others bustled around her, Elisabeth studied the asymmetrical house with its bay windows, balconies, stained glass, turrets, porches, brackets and ornamental masonry. The structure was two-storied, except for a third floor at the top of one pointed turret. That was the room where she and her sisters had spent hours reading and dreaming. She still used the space to relax and find a peaceful spot away from the boys.

Elisabeth exhaled with relief at being safely home.

She found her bags just inside her doorway where Gil had set them. She needed to unpack. Father would have duties piled up for her.

Sweat trickled along his spine, but the bandanna he'd tied around his head beneath his black cowboy hat kept perspiration from his eyes. Vision was critical when a keen eye meant the difference between life and death.

Gabe studied the cabin baking beneath the blistering sun. The man he'd been hunting for the past six weeks was holed up in there with a bottle of whiskey and a slug in his thigh. If he hadn't passed out from pain or bled to death, heat and starvation would drive him out eventually. Gabe rested his rifle against a bolder and reached for his canteen. Empty? He'd only just filled it. His throat was burning and dry; he needed water badly.

Heat more searing than the sun licked up his side. The dry grass around him was on fire! He jumped up to escape the flames and a shot rang out. His prey had exited the cabin and aimed another shot at Gabe, now standing and exposed.

Gabe reached for his rifle. It was gone, and in its place a coiled rattler lifted its head and shook its tail in warning.

Gabe jerked awake.

He lay drenched with sweat and his side throbbed. His tongue felt too big for his mouth. For a moment he didn't recognize the room, but then the train robbery and his subsequent ride to the doctor's home came back to him.

"He's one stubborn fellow." Vaguely, Gabe remembered the doctor removing the bullet from his side, but now instead of a blood-spattered apron, the man was wearing a clean white shirt and tie.

"Heavy, too." The black-haired fellow beside him threaded his hair back from his forehead and stared down.

Grimacing, Gabe raised up on one elbow.

"No more getting out of this bed," the doctor ordered and poured a glass of water from a nearby pitcher. He had silver hair at his temples, but was probably only ten years older than Gabe.

That's right. He'd made a foolhardy attempt to use the outhouse on his own. Gabe gulped down four glasses of the cool liquid before he lay back. "How long was I out?"

"You blacked out when I removed the bullet yesterday. It cracked your rib, but traveled a ways. Now stay put or I'll tie you to this bed. Good thing the reverend came along or I'd never have gotten you back in here."

Reverend? "Am I dying?"

"You're not dying," Matthew Barnes assured him. "You're just weak from losing so much blood. You need to rest and build up your strength."

"Why'd you call the preacher?"

"He didn't call me." The man offered his hand. "I'm Samuel Hart. My daughter was on the train yesterday. She's one of the passengers you saved from being robbed. She told me all about the incident."

"Hart," he said with a scowl. "The blonde?"

"That's Elisabeth."

Gabe groaned. "She had a strong aversion to parting with her neck chain."

Samuel Hart nodded. "She's worn the ring on that chain ever since my first wife died."

Gabe glanced around the room, finally noting there was another man lying on a cot several feet away. He looked to be sleeping or unconscious. "What's wrong with him?"

"Snake bite," Dr. Barnes replied. "Just got here an hour or so ago."

Gabe turned his attention back to the preacher. "If the doc didn't call you, why are you here?"

"I came yesterday, too, though you never woke up. I prayed for you and came back to see how you're doing."

Gabe couldn't recall anyone praying over him before. "I hurt like I've been dragged behind a team of horses."

The man in the other bed moaned, and the doctor moved to attend to him.

"Well, thank God you're alive," the preacher said.

Gabe studied him again and attempted to sit up, but pain lanced through his side and took his breath away. He rested a hand over the bandages. "I've been shot before, but it never hurt like this."

"Cracked ribs hurt more than a wound," the doctor said. "But you can't take a chance on opening that hole or letting it get infected."

"I can't stay here," Gabe objected. For one thing, if any of the train robbers' friends had heard of him being shot, the first place they'd search would be the doctor's. "I have business to see to."

"Where do you plan to go?" the doc asked him. "You need close supervision for at least a week or better."

"Looks like you've got your hands full with the snake-bit fella," Gabe replied.

"You can come home with me," the preacher said.

Gabe gave him a sidelong look.

"I have a big house full of women who can help me look out for you."

"I do have to head out this afternoon and make calls," the doc advised. "Plus look after this fella. You'd likely get better care at the Harts'."

Gabe hated to admit it, but the thought of moving more than his toes made him sweat. He'd pulled through a lot worse than this, though. "All right. The preacher's house it is."

Chapter Three

Elisabeth returned from the clothesline with a basket of her clean folded clothing in time to hear a commotion coming from the front hall.

"Not there!" a man shouted. "Don't grab me there, for pity's sake!"

She didn't recognize the voice, but then her father's more calming words reached her. "We'll have you settled in just a minute, Mr. Taggart."

Taggart? She entered the enormous sunlit foyer from the back hallway, stopped and stared.

Her father and Gil supported the tall man, one on each side, and Dr. Barnes followed, carrying his bag in one hand, a carton in the other.

"Just a little farther," Sam coaxed.

"Any farther and you might as well just shoot me again," the man growled. Sweat beaded on his forehead and his swarthy face had turned pasty white. A steep set of narrow stairs led from the street up to the house, and he'd just maneuvered them with a bullet wound.

Sam glanced up. "Elisabeth, bring cold water and wash rags to the bedroom on the south corner."

"But that's..." At her father's stern look, she let her voice trail off. *Next to mine*. What was he thinking? "Yes, sir."

She set down her basket and hurried to the kitchen. Her father had brought that man here! To their home! She cringed in mortification. Now she'd be forced to face him—*and* her shame.

Minutes later, she climbed the stairs with a pitcher and toweling. She traveled the now-silent corridor and paused outside the closed door. From inside, she heard rustles and a couple of grunts.

The door opened and her father gestured for her to enter.

Gil stood just inside the room, and she met his interested gaze. "Looks like Mr. Taggart's going to be your guest for a while," he said.

Reluctantly, she followed her father inside.

They had removed the man's clothing and tucked a sheet up around his waist and over part of his chest. His ribs were bound, the white wrapping a stark contrast against dark skin that held scars from previous injuries. Who *was* this man?

"You did just fine," Dr. Barnes said, standing over him. "The wound isn't bleeding." He turned and took the pitcher from Elisabeth, poured water into the bowl and got a cloth wet. "The Harts will take care of you. They're good people."

Gabe took the wet rag from the doctor and wiped his perspiring face.

Dr. Barnes set a bottle on the bureau. "He gets two teaspoons every six hours for pain. It'll help him sleep. Give him a dose now."

"You'll be in charge of his medicine, Elisabeth," her father directed.

"Me-e?" She hadn't meant to squeak.

"You're the most meticulous," he replied.

She nodded her obedient consent, but kept the disagreeable man she'd hoped never to see again under her observation. He didn't appear any more pleased with the situation than she, which was a comfort.

"I'll check on you tomorrow," the doc told him.

Gil glanced from the stranger to Elisabeth with a crooked grin and headed downstairs, followed by the doctor.

"Elisabeth will see to your needs," Sam told Gabe. "And I'll be back at suppertime."

He progressed into the hall, and she followed, not wanting to be left alone with their patient. The other two men headed downstairs. "What am I supposed to do with him?" she whispered to her father.

"Give him his medicine and something to drink. Let him sleep. If he gets hungry, bring him a meal." He took a step toward the stairs, but stopped and met her gaze. "Oh, and you might try thanking him for saving your mother's wedding ring."

He turned and walked away.

Her heart picked up speed and, as though the pressure would calm her pulse, she flattened her palm against her waist. She took a deep breath and released it. Slowly, she turned back to the room and entered, lowering the hand to her side. The Taggart fellow leveled that piercing green gaze on her, but his demeanor was blessedly less imposing minus his hat and shirt.

"Alone at last," he said.

Normally she prided herself on her calm demeanor, but this man managed to fluster her with every breath.

"Where did they put my gun?"

"You're not going to need your gun here," she assured him.

Grimacing, he attempted to lean forward, but grabbed his side through the sheet and bandage. "It's on that bureau." He pointed. "Bring it here."

Rather than argue with him, she stepped to the chest of drawers and picked up the surprisingly heavy tooled leather holster that sheathed the deadly looking weapon. He'd shot half a dozen bandits in the blink of an eye with this very gun. Holding it on both upturned palms, she carried it to him.

Meeting her eyes first, and making her even more uncomfortable with his stare, he took the belt from her. Yanking the gun from the its sheath, he swiftly opened the cylinder and fed bullets plucked from the belt into the chambers. After flipping the cylinder closed and sliding the gun under the pillow behind his head, he let the holster fall to the floor.

"I'll go fetch a spoon and a water glass." She couldn't get out of that room fast enough. Elisabeth stood in the kitchen longer than necessary, finding reasons to delay. What kind of man loaded a gun and stashed it under his pillow? What—or who—did he expect to shoot here? He hadn't been wearing a badge or a star, but just carrying a gun didn't make him a criminal. Her own father had worn a gun during their travels west and for months after arriving in Jackson Springs.

Finally, she returned and measured a dose from the liquid in the brown bottle. "Would you like a drink?"

"I'd love a drink, lady, but I'll settle for that water." Grimacing, he rose on one elbow to take the glass and finish the water. "Thanks."

Noticing the sun arrowing through the shutters, she closed them and pulled the curtains closed over both windows, leaving the room dim.

"I never asked where you were headed." She wrung out the cloth and hung it on the towel bar attached to the washstand.

"Here."

"Oh." She came to stand beside the bed. "Do you have family in Jackson Springs?"

"I own some land," he replied. "I'm going to buy horses and build a house. Might buy a business or two."

"What type of business?"

"Depends on what's for sale."

She had to wonder if he had any skills or definite plans or if he'd just set off willy-nilly. "I see." She left and returned with a small brass bell. "Ring if you need anything."

Her father's suggestion burned. She reached to place a hand over the ring that lay under her bodice and, even though the room was only semi-lit, Gabe's astute perusal followed.

He had protected her from harm, saved her ring and

had become injured in the process. Why did she have so much difficulty forming the words?

"Thank you, Mr. Taggart."

He curled his lip. "That wasn't so hard, was it?"

Irritating man. She spun and fled.

"He's wike Wyatt Eawp."

"Where's his six-shooter?" another child asked. "Jimmy Fuller said he shot the robbers with a six-shooter."

Gabe rolled his woozy head toward the open door and caught sight of three little boys. They scattered like chicks in the wake of a bantam rooster, and Elisabeth Hart entered with a laden tray.

In disbelief, he blinked sleep from his eyes. "You have *kids?*"

Elisabeth frowned. "I'm barely twenty years old, Mr. Taggart." She set the tray on the bureau and opened the curtains, the thick blond braid hanging down her back swaying with her movements. She slid the window open wider. "Those are my young brothers."

He blinked at the glare of the late-afternoon light, but the breeze gusting in was most welcome. The sheet stuck to his skin and he plucked it loose. "Your father only mentioned daughters."

Gabe hadn't thought she looked old enough to have all those kids, but looks were often deceiving. She stepped close to arrange the pillows behind him. He sat forward with her scent, a combination of freshly ironed linen and meadow grass, enveloping him. He hadn't expected the alarming effect she had on his senses. He scratched his chin. "He said there was a house full of females."

"My sisters have come home from school, but they have lessons to complete. My stepmother needs her rest, so…" She snapped open a napkin and draped it over his chest. "You're stuck with me." She uncovered the plate of food and carried the bed tray to him. "I prepared a roast while you slept, along with potatoes and carrots. Beef will build up your strength."

Spotting the plate of food and the savory aroma of meat and gravy made his belly rumble. At least she could cook. He picked up the fork in anticipation. "I haven't eaten anything that looked half this appetizin' in a long while."

"I'm not the cook my stepmother is, but I'm not half-bad. My skills lie in accounting and organization, but I can do most anything I set my mind to."

He took a bite and savored the taste of the tender roast. She could cook *well*. "You're used to getting your way."

She studied him and shrugged. "I see that things get done."

He ate several bites, then pointed at the nearby wooden chair with his fork. "Where were you returnin' from when we met?"

Stiffly, she seated herself. "Morning Creek. I'm the notary public for this county."

"Unusual job for a female." He couldn't say he was surprised. She seemed anything but usual, and her persnickety ways probably made her good with details.

"The position fell into my lap after an elderly parish-

ioner passed away a year ago. The post required someone willing to travel to nearby towns once a month or
so." She raised one shoulder in a delicate shrug. "The
job sounded like a good way to do a bit of traveling.
And it has been. Until yesterday." A frown formed between her pale eyebrows. "Nothing like the incident on
the train has happened before."

Her perfect speech amused him. "So the body count's
been low until now."

She averted her attention to the window, and he was
almost sorry for the jibe. Almost. "Ruffle your tail
feathers, don't I?"

She swung her attention back. "You're the first person
I ever met who is deliberately antagonistic. Why do you
do that?"

Her directness did surprise him. The females he'd
known invariably played coy and solicitous. "I'm not
the one who provoked a robber holding a loaded .45."

She lifted her chin to say, "I was going to give him
the ring. I was ready to take it off and hand it over."

"So you say now."

Her blue eyes flashed with aggravation. "I'm not a
liar, Mr. Taggart."

Amused, he set down his fork and reached for the
cup of coffee. It was strong and black, the best he'd
tasted in a long time.

She delved into the pocket of her apron, withdrew
a timepiece and glanced at it. She stood. "It's time for
your medicine."

And then he'd sleep again. He didn't like the vulnerability of being unconscious for hours at a time. He

tested the pain by raising his arm, then glanced at the forested mountainside visible from the windows she'd opened. "This place looks to be set against a foothill," he said when she approached with the spoon and bottle of medicine. "Is there a main road close by?"

"No. Just the mountain behind us," she replied. "And a few homes farther down the hillside. Only one street leads up here." The Hart home stood silhouetted against the lush green pines and above most of the town, protected by the shadow of the mountain.

"I'll pass on the medicine this time." He reached for his coffee again, wincing at the pain that shot through his ribs. "And I'd be obliged if you'd run an errand on my behalf."

Her expression hinted at reluctance. "It's the least I can do. What's the task?"

"I need you to inquire about taxes on my land."

She set away the bottle of medicine. "You'll be settling here then."

"Jackson Springs strikes me as a quiet place."

"What did you do before?"

"Traveled." He set down his cup. "The roast was tasty. Thanks."

She picked up his tray. "That wasn't so hard, was it?"

"I'm grateful for the care, no matter how begrudgingly it's given."

She ignored that comment. "I'll visit the real estate office tomorrow. Is there anything else you need?"

He shook his head.

She headed for the door. "I'll check on you later."

Gabe reached to move a pillow from behind his back and winced. He lay back as gently as he could. The house was silent, save for a clock ticking somewhere.

He didn't like lying around, and neither did he cotton to having the Hart woman waiting on him. Besides the fact that he didn't like her seeing him this way, he had things to do. He needed to find a place to live before his sister, Irene, got here in another four weeks. That should have been plenty of time, but now...

He hadn't counted on this setback.

As far as anyone knew he was a businessman here to establish himself in a new community and settle into a normal life. So far nothing had gone according to plan, but he could get things back on track.

Without the pain medicine, he slept fitfully. At the sound of a feminine voice, he again woke with the damp sheets sticking to his skin and his head throbbing.

"I'm sorry to disturb you, but the marshal is here to see you." It was her. Still looking fresh and irritatingly healthy. Maybe it was the drugging effect of the medicine on his head, but the woman was downright pretty.

"Is there water in that bowl over there?" He attempted to sit and swing his legs over the side of the bed, but at the pain in his side, lay back against the pillows. "I need to wash up."

Elisabeth noted the full bowl and arranged toweling on the washstand, then turned back to him. "Can I help you?"

"Send one of the lads in."

She glanced toward the door and back at him with a look of concern. "The oldest is only six."

"He can fetch for me. Unless you want to stick around while I get my pants on."

She stared at him without flinching; he had to give her credit for that. But then with a swish of skirts and petticoats, she turned to where his satchel sat against a wall. As she leaned to grab the handles, her braid swung over her shoulder. She hoisted the bag onto the bench at the foot of the bed and opened it. "I'll get Phillip." She looked Gabe square in the eye. "And then I will stand right outside that door where I can hear everything."

"Suit yourself." What did she think he was going to do? Give the boy shooting lessons? "Stand right here if you want to."

She left the room with her back ramrod-straight and returned a few minutes later to usher in a handsome black-haired little fella with freckles. He surveyed Gabe with curious wide blue eyes.

"This is my brother, Phillip," Elisabeth said. "Phillip, Mr. Taggart needs help getting up and dressing. I'll be right out in the hall." She glanced from her brother to Gabe and backed out, leaving the door open a full twelve inches.

"Thanks for comin' to my rescue," Gabe told him. "Think you could help me stand without pullin' on my left arm?"

"Sure!" Phillip hopped right up on the bed and got behind Gabe to push him upward.

Gabe did his best not to grunt or groan. He'd eat dirt before he'd show weakness in front of the boy—or the woman listening outside the door. He wrapped the sheet around his waist and stood, making his way over to the bowl of water. His reflection in the mirror revealed several days' worth of whiskers on his cheeks and chin. He scratched at it and poured water into the basin. "Can you find the roll of toiletries in my bag there? I need my razor."

Phillip found the roll and carried the supplies to the stand, where a shaving brush and mug sat at the ready. Gabe used water and powder to make lather and dabbed it on his face.

"My papa gots a black beard, too."

Gabe gave an unintelligible reply as he drew the razor up his neck and chin.

"I'm getting one, too."

Gabe eyeballed him in the mirror. "Might be a year or two before you need to shave."

"I'm gonna grow stubble like you."

"Ladies like a stubble," he replied.

"Mr. Taggart," Elisabeth cautioned from the hall-way.

"Tickles when you kiss 'em," he added.

Phillip pulled a face. "I'm not gonna kiss girls."

"Mr. Taggart!" she warned more loudly.

He washed, wet his hair and used his brush and comb. "Can you find me a clean shirt and trousers?"

Phillip set himself to the task. Then the boy leaped up to stand on the bench and held out the shirt so Gabe could ease into it. "Is it true you shot all those robbers who tried to steal ever'body's jewelry?"

Gabe paused in guiding his arm through the sleeve

and looked at the child. "Sometimes takin' another man's life is the only choice. But it's never an easy choice and never something to be proud of."

"Did you ever shoot anyone before that?"

Gabe buttoned his shirt without reply. Phillip helped him don a clean pair of trousers. "Can you pick that up for me?" he asked, and the lad grabbed his holster from the floor and handed it to him. Gabe showed him how to hold it up so he could get it over one shoulder and around his ribs without touching the side that pained him. He took his Colt from under the pillow and slid it into the holster.

Phillip's eyes widened. "Is that the gun you used?"

"Yep. Has your pa taught you about guns?"

The boy nodded. "Yes, sir. I ain't apposed to touch one until I'm bigger. Not Papa's gun, either."

Gabe absorbed the information.

"You're a top-notch valet." He flipped him a coin.

Phillip caught it. "What's a valet?"

"A fellow who helps a gentleman get dressed. Can't say as I ever had the need before, but I'm fortunate you were here. I wouldn't have wanted to endanger your sister's sensibilities." Gabe leaned close and whispered, "She's a good cook, but she's prickly."

Phillip grinned.

"Are you decent?" Elisabeth called from the other side of the door. She didn't like the sound of that man whispering to her brother.

The door whisked open and he stood in the opening in a clean, albeit wrinkled shirt, his dark hair combed into sleek waves. He wore the leather holster with his loaded gun tucked against his good side.

She'd never faced him standing before. He was a good foot taller than she was and filled the doorway with his imposing presence. One side of his mouth quirked up and her traitorous thoughts raced to his remarks about kissing ladies.

"I'll get the marshal," she said.

"No. I'll come down."

He was a stubborn one, that was for sure. "Phillip," she instructed. "Walk on Mr. Taggart's other side."

"I'd crush the boy if I fell on him," he scoffed. "Thanks for your help, Phil. Run along and come back tonight, all right?"

"All right!" The lad tossed a coin in the air and shot toward his room.

She accompanied their antagonistic guest to the parlor, where Roy Dalton waited. He shook Gabe's hand. "Taggart?" he asked.

Gabe turned to Elisabeth. "Thank you."

She blinked in surprise. She'd been promptly dismissed in her own home. She turned and left to find Josie and Abigail in the kitchen.

"Goodness, you fixed an entire meal while I napped," Josie said. "I had so much energy when I woke that I'm making pies. Abigail is helping me."

Elisabeth's younger sister had learned to bake and cook at Josie's side, and her desserts rivaled any that the ladies of the church produced.

"Did you remember that the Jacksons will be here for supper?" Abigail asked.

"I forgot." Elisabeth glanced at her stepmother. "Will there be enough food?"

"We'll serve your roast, and we can add more potatoes and carrots and maybe a slaw," Josie answered.

"Mr. Jackson likes roast beef," Abigail remarked. At seventeen, she thought Rhys Jackson's presence at dinner was exceedingly romantic. Elisabeth was far too practical to be caught up in such silly imaginings.

As the preacher, her father invited members from the congregation for dinner at least once a week. It had been Josie's desire to make a home where they could entertain and where their neighbors would feel welcome. The Jacksons ate with them more often than most other families. Beatrice was a widow, but a well-to-do widow, and her son Rhys worked at the bank. Elisabeth suspected that their recurring invitations had something to do with the fact that Rhys was an eligible, well-mannered bachelor.

Her father and Josie had never said they were impatient for her to marry and leave their home, so perhaps the new concern she'd been feeling was only her imagination. The house certainly wasn't too crowded for her to remain. In fact, bringing Kalli into their midst had added yet another person to the household and the dinner table. She wasn't a burden on her parents.

"Do you suppose Mr. Taggart and the marshal would care for a glass of lemonade?" Josie asked.

Elisabeth glanced at Josie's flour-covered hands as she shaped the piecrust and then gave her sister a hopeful look. Abigail sprinkled cinnamon on her sliced apples without looking up. "I'll pour them lemonade," she finally offered.

She set out two glasses. "Josie? Do you feel I contribute to the family?"

"Contribute?" Josie looked up. "You are an important part of this family, Elisabeth. Why would you ask such a question?"

She shrugged off her insecurity. "No reason. Forget I asked."

Sometime later, she carried a tray into the parlor and set it on the serving cart. The men's conversation ground to a halt. She set a frosty glass in front of each of them on a low table before the settee. Gabe looked decidedly out of place on the dainty piece of furniture.

"Miss Hart, will you join us, please?" Roy Dalton asked.

Surprised, she recovered her composure and seated herself on a chair opposite the marshal.

"Mr. Taggart isn't willing to accept the entire sum of the reward money."

Startled, she glanced at Gabe and back. "There is a reward?"

"Three of those fellas were wanted in several states for train robberies," he replied. "And two of them for murder."

"Oh, my." Clasping her hands together, she silently thanked God. They'd all come dangerously close to losing their lives. She remembered the verse in the Psalms that talked about God giving His angels charge over her, and knew it was so.

"Mr. Taggart claims he can't take all the credit for catching those men."

"Meaning that God had a hand in what happened?" She looked to Gabe, but he didn't reply.

The marshal was still holding his hat, and he turned it around by the brim. "Seems he's of the mind that you were the one responsible for insisting he do something about their apprehension."

"Oh, he is." She bored her gaze into Gabe's and then couldn't resist a glance at the gun he wore.

"Claims he would've handed over his valuables and let those good-for-nothin's go on their merry way if you hadn't started the ruckus."

Anger burned a fiery path to Elisabeth's cheeks, but she didn't look away.

"Mr. Taggart's a real generous and honest fella. Half the reward money is yours." The marshal took a fat envelope made from folded parchment from the settee cushion beside him and shoved it toward her. "This here's your share."

She held the packet in both hands before she realized what had just happened. "What is this?"

"Half the reward money, like I said," Roy replied.

Reward. For killing those men? Elisabeth dropped the envelope as though it was a poisonous snake. The seams of the envelope burst open and a stack of currency spread across the rug.

Blood money.

Chapter Four

"I don't want that!" Elisabeth sized up the marshal and then Gabe. "I'm not accepting money for those men's deaths."

"That's what reward money is," Roy replied. He knelt and scooped up the scattered bills and tucked them back in order and closed the paper over them. He extended the package. "It's your half."

"But I didn't do anything," she objected. "I didn't hold a gun."

"They'd have gotten clean away with everyone's purses and watches if you hadn't caused a ruckus," Gabe disagreed. "I gave the bandit mine." His gaze fell to the chain at her neck, though the ring was beneath her bodice like always. "Your kinship with your jewelry set the whole episode in motion. So half is yours."

"Well, I won't take it."

Gabe raised a brow and looked at Roy. "What happens to the money if she won't take it?"

The marshal pursed his lips and scratched his chin

with a thumb. "Don't reckon I know. It's never happened before. Goes back in the city coffers, I guess."

"Shame all that cash goin' to waste," Gabe remarked. "Could've bought your brothers shoes or hired your father a hand or…" Gabe appeared thoughtful, then pleased with himself. "You could have taken a trip somewhere."

"My brothers have all the shoes they need, thank you, and I am my father's assistant." She paused, however, considering that a trip might have been nice. But that was vain and selfish thinking. She could have given the money to the church to provide help to those in need.

Could have? She still could. Elisabeth extended her palm. "I'll take it."

Seeming pleased not to have to deal with the money, Roy handed over the packet.

"I'll give it to the church," she decided.

"It's yours to do with as you see fit," Gabe said with a shrug.

"Well, that takes care of the business I came to do." Roy finished his lemonade and excused himself. She showed the sheriff to the door, then returned to the sitting room.

Elisabeth held the envelope to her chest. The Taggart fellow's face looked paler than it had been, and he'd set his mouth in a grim line. He was quite obviously in pain and too stubborn to say so. "You should've let me bring the marshal upstairs so you didn't have to dress and come down."

"I needed to move a bit." He stood, but swayed on his feet.

She tucked the money in her apron pocket and hurried to his side. "Lean on me."

"I can manage."

"I said lean on me, Mr. Taggart. If you fall flat on your face, I'll never get you up by myself."

He seemed to consider that as a distinct possibility and wrapped one solid arm across her shoulders.

With him butted up against her side, his imposing height and hard muscle were glaringly obvious. Now the possibility of him falling and crushing her became the issue. "Phillip!" she called.

A minute later, her brother skidded to a stop in front of them.

"Get on the other side of Mr. Taggart and do your best to help me get him to the banister where he can hold on."

Phillip eyed the holster, but ducked obediently under Gabe's other arm, and they managed their way to the front hall, where Gabe grabbed the banister and helped support his weight.

"Don't get behind us," Elisabeth warned. "Run ahead."

Phillip scampered up the stairs.

The farther they climbed, the more Gabe leaned his weight against her, until, at the top, she feared they'd both topple down the stairs. With Herculean effort, she used every ounce of her strength to keep him upright. "Come back and get his other side!" she called to Phillip.

The boy was a minimal help, though his face turned red from his efforts.

"Mr. Taggart, you're going to have to help or we're going to drop you in a heap right here," she huffed.

Lifting his head, he rose to the occasion with a grunt and they made it through the correct doorway and to the bed, where they dropped him unceremoniously.

He lay atop the blankets, his face white, his eyelashes lying against his cheeks.

"This is ridiculous," she said, straightening her skirts and her disheveled hair, while catching her breath. "You're taking your medicine and sleeping and not getting back out of bed until you're better able."

She poured a dose of the liquid painkiller, and with Phillip's help got it down Gabe's throat, then got him situated on the bed and closed the curtains.

"Is he dead?" Phillip asked.

"No, he's breathing," she answered, but paused to watch his chest rise and fall. "He's sleeping."

"He's sleeping in his clothes," the boy remarked. "And wearing his holster and gun."

"That's his own fault. He could have stayed put and he'd still be comfortable." Her hand went to the thick envelope in her apron pocket. Just having all that money on her person made her uncomfortable. She would give the ill-gotten gains to her father and let him use it to his discretion. She led Phillip out of the room. "We'll let him be."

She carried the money to Sam's study and left it in his top desk drawer, then hurried to the kitchen to help Josie with supper.

The Jacksons were again their guests at dinner that evening. Beatrice had been a widow for the past five years and occupied herself holding tea parties and peddling her son as a perspective husband. From all accounts it looked as though Elisabeth was her first choice. Beatrice raised a questioning brow at her now. "Elisabeth, we were quite concerned when we heard the news about the holdup and learned that you'd been on the train. How dreadful for you. Thank the good Lord you weren't injured."

"I'm thanking God for my safety," Elisabeth replied, not wanting to talk about the incident.

"Mr. Taggart saved Lis'beth," Phillip piped up. "And he saved all the people's watches and rings and money, too. Din't he, Lis'beth?" He sat with a slice of turnip forgotten on the tines of his fork, his expression serious. "He gots a big gun."

Beatrice's eyes widened. Rhys glanced from Phillip to Elisabeth.

Samuel Hart spoke up, saying, "We're all appreciative for Elisabeth's safe return home."

Josie returned to the dining room at that moment. Elisabeth took the refilled bowl of mashed potatoes and reached to set it in the middle of the table. Unconsciously, Josie spread her hand at the small of her back before taking her seat. Elisabeth glanced at Rhys at that moment, confused by the fleeting expression that darkened his features before quickly disappearing.

She'd gone to school with Rhys, though he'd finished ahead of her. He'd always been interested in the Harts and enjoyed coming to their home. He worked at the bank and knew much of the goings-on of the townspeople.

"Does your new position sit well with you, Miss Tyler?" Beatrice asked.

Kalli had been assigned a seat between Peter and John, where she sliced their meat and encouraged them to eat their vegetables. She glanced up. "Yes, ma'am. Quite well."

"Kalli is a perfect fit for our family," Josie added.

Elisabeth glanced at her sisters to note any reactions to Josie's remark. Anna was absorbed in her meal, and Abigail was giving Rhys surreptitious glances. Neither seemed to think anything of Kalli's presence or the conversation.

Anna glanced up and smiled, and with a surge of affection, Elisabeth returned the smile. She dearly loved her sisters. They shared so much history, and wonderful memories of their mother.

Sam had brought Elisabeth and her sisters to Jackson Springs after their mother's death and his remarriage to Josie. Elisabeth had been filling the role of caregiver and nurturer and at first felt usurped by Josie's new position as her stepmother. But it hadn't been easy to resent a woman so kind and generous and who made her sisters happy. She and Josie had come to an understanding, and she had grown to love the woman dearly.

Still, even though their marriage and family had turned out well, Elisabeth sometimes questioned her father marrying for convenience. She was far from a romantic—in fact she was a painfully logical and practical person—yet Elisabeth had always imagined herself finding a love born of common interests, mutual needs and future plans. She wanted to marry for love and passion, not practicality.

Her father had never questioned Elisabeth's choice to assist him in his duties, appreciating in fact, that she took care of details and finances while he saw to the spiritual and emotional needs of his congregation. Still, it was the natural order of life for a man or woman to leave her father and mother and marry.

She had turned twenty on her last birthday. Most of the young ladies with whom she'd attended school were married and already had their own children. Elisabeth loved her young brothers and had spent a good share of time caring for them. Perhaps that was why she hadn't yet experienced a burning desire to have her own children.

Once she was married she'd undoubtedly feel different. Love changed everything. Zebediah Turner had called on her for a season. She'd been to his family's ranch with her father a time or two. When Zeb had kissed her after an ice cream social, their relationship had grown awkward. He hadn't called on her again, and he later married someone from Morning Creek.

Studying Rhys now, she wondered about the whole kissing thing. Maybe it just had to be the right person.

"How was school today?" Josie asked, looking to Abigail and Anna.

"I finished all my assignments in class," Abigail replied. "So I have no studies this evening. I'd like to make pies with those apples Mr. Stone gave Papa, if that's all right."

"No one around here ever objects to pie," Josie answered with a smile.

"I have arithmetic to finish," Anna said. "May I sit in your study with you, Papa?"

The sound of a bell tinkled from a distance. It took a second for Elisabeth to process the sound. She set down her fork. "Excuse me."

"Can I come help Mr. Taggart with you, Lis'beth?" Phillip asked.

Rhys set down his fork and studied her with a questioning look.

"Your sister can handle it," Sam said to Phillip. "Eat your turnips."

"The man is *here?*" Beatrice asked. "In your home?"

"He was injured defending my daughter and many passengers," Sam told her. "The least we could do was offer him a place to recuperate. My wife wanted this great big house so we could be a blessing to others. Over the years we've had a goodly amount of guests stay with us."

Beatrice blotted her lips with her napkin.

"He was sleeping the last time I checked on him," Elisabeth told Josie. "I imagine he's awake and hungry."

"I made him a plate," Josie answered. "It's in the warmer."

In the kitchen, Elisabeth readied a tray and carried it up the back stairs.

"I could've come down," Gabe said when he saw

her. He had managed a sitting position with the pillows behind his shoulders.

"That didn't go so well last time." She set the tray on his lap. He was still fully dressed, boots and all.

"You knocked me out." Frowning, he picked up the fork and tasted the potatoes.

She stood at the foot of the bed. "You're easier to get along with that way."

"You're amusing, but it's not safe for me to be unconscious."

"And why is that?"

"Train robbers have friends. And relatives. If word got out that the man who shot their friends was staying here, they might come looking for me."

"Nothing will happen to you while you're in this home."

He raised a brow. "Didn't see any armed guards when I got here."

"Our shield and fortress isn't visible to the eye. Psalm ninety-one assures us that God has given His angels charge over us to protect us in all our ways."

He looked at her as though she'd just told him she could fly. "In my experience the only sure thing is something I can see and feel."

He stabbed a bite of meat and chewed it.

"Your limited experience doesn't change the truth," she answered.

Gabe looked at the woman. Really studied her. She was as prickly as they came, opinionated and unafraid of speaking her mind—even if her head was full of foolishness. But she was something to look at, that was for sure.

He'd thought so ever since she'd walked down the aisle of that railcar, looking for an empty seat and finding only the one beside him. Her hair was the palest shade he'd ever set eyes upon outside a field of summer wheat. Tonight she didn't have it braided, but gathered away from her temples and trailing down her back like a schoolgirl's.

Her delicate features belied her bold statements and cutting barbs, a juxtaposition he rather enjoyed for its uniqueness.

She was slender, but not skinny, with curves in all the right places. She wore a burgundy-colored skirt with a flounce of some sort in the back. Her fitted ivory blouse was printed with flowers the same color as her skirt and the rounded neck opening revealed the chain that held her gold ring.

She caught him looking at it and brought her hand up to touch the piece of jewelry.

"Medicine wore off, and it was awfully quiet," he said.

"We were having dinner."

He imagined the whole family around a table. "You can go on back."

"Are you certain you don't mind? We do have guests."

"Any pretty young ladies?"

"No, Mr. Taggart. A widow and her son."

"A pretty widow woman?" he asked.

She frowned. "'Beauty is vain, but a woman that feareth the Lord, she shall be praised.'"

"From the Bible?"

She nodded.

"What about you? You're pretty."

Pink tinged her cheeks, the only indication that his question had affected her. "I prefer to be appreciated for my abilities."

"So, you know you're pretty?"

"You're impertinent, Mr. Taggart."

"No disrespect intended. Most ladies enjoy a compliment." He dug back into his meal. "Your father said he had a houseful of women, and seems they're all good cooks."

"Leave your tray on the end of the bed when you're finished." She turned and left the room.

He stared at the spot she'd vacated for a long moment. Her idealism stood firm in the safe cocoon of her protected world, but one of these days when faced with a reality she couldn't pray her way out of, Elisabeth Hart was in for a big disappointment.

For some reason he couldn't explain, he hoped he wasn't around to see it.

Chapter Five

The following morning, Gabe found a pitcher of water outside his door, carried and poured it into the bowl on the washstand. It irritated him that the wound in his side was so debilitating, even to the point of making it painful to raise his arm.

After washing and shaving, he dressed and opened the door. Minutes later, Elisabeth appeared. "My father has excused me from my duties for a few days in order to look after you." Her tone relayed her displeasure in the fact. She extended a piece of paper. "I got to the land office early. This is how much you owe."

She'd obviously seen the amount, since the paper wasn't folded or in an envelope. He glanced up, noting her almost pleased expression.

He cocked an eyebrow. "Guess that will take care of my share of the reward money." Did she think that was all he had to his name? He went to the bureau, took out his packet of money and counted it. He extended all but a few bills. "That'll cover the taxes."

She took the money.

"One more thing."

She met his gaze, and her eyes reminded him of a clear mountain lake.

"I'm going to need a place to live until I can build." It was probably going to be a few weeks before he could work much himself, but he could hire someone to get the house started.

"I'll see what I can do." She turned back toward the hall. "I'll bring your breakfast and then run your errands."

While he ate, a dark-haired woman tapped on the open door. "Mr. Taggart? I thought it was about time I came to introduce myself. I'm Josie Hart."

"Pleased to make your acquaintance, ma'am. You're a fine cook, and I thank you for lettin' me stay here."

"You're most welcome." She was a pretty woman with a friendly smile and the girth of an expected new life under her white apron. "I climb the stairs as few times as possible during the day, so I wanted to stop by now."

"Pleased you did."

"How is your injury?"

"More bother than I'd like, but I'll be fine."

"Elisabeth has gone downtown, so I'll be listening for your bell, and I'll have Phillip come if you ring."

"Shouldn't need anything, ma'am."

Elisabeth had mentioned her stepmother. That was why Elisabeth looked nothing like this woman…and why she set such store by that ring around her neck. Her own mother had died.

He knew what it was like to lose a parent. He'd lost

both of his when he'd been sixteen and Irene barely ten. He'd tried working two jobs, but it had been no life for a little girl, so he'd hired on with a cattle drive and left his sister in the best place he could find.

It hadn't taken long for him to learn there was more money to be earned hunting bounties than punching cows. Before long Irene was in one of the best boarding schools in Pennsylvania and he was earning a name for himself.

Now nineteen, his sister had been after him to bring her to live with him. In order to do that, he needed to make a new start, make a home for her and leave his past behind.

Irene didn't know what he'd done all those years. He'd led her to believe he'd made enough herding cows to invest and create a tidy nest egg. She would never know the truth as long as he had his way. And he always had his way. He'd be the most respectable man she could ask for in a brother, and he'd see to it she found a husband worthy of her.

If it wasn't for this bullet hole in his side, he'd be buying lumber and roofing nails right this minute. The frustration of this setback ate at him. He wasn't used to relying on other people.

Especially not persnickety women.

He checked his revolver and tucked it into its holster against his side.

"My ma sent me for the tray."

Gabe turned at Phillip's voice.

Eyeing him, the boy picked up the meal tray. "I gotta go to school."

Gabe nodded and gave him a silent salute.

He shouldn't have been so blasted tired just from getting up and shaving, but winded, he lay back down. He'd been sleeping a short time when footsteps woke him.

Elisabeth was turning away to leave.

"I'm awake."

She stopped and turned back. She held a sheaf of papers. "This is your deed and your proof of taxes paid."

After handing it to him, she opened the curtains and the shutters so he could look over the papers. After a cursory glance, he set them down. "Appreciate it."

She looked away and then back. "There are homes for sale here and there. The boardinghouse has an opening. There's a room over the tailor's for rent."

"I need a little more room than that. A small house would do."

"Well, there is one small house. It's at the bottom of the hill, just down from here, and it's vacant."

"I'll take that then."

"Don't you want to see it first?"

"I can hire someone to clean it."

"That won't be necessary. The church owns it and takes care of the upkeep. I'll let my father know you'll be renting it."

"As soon as the doctor says I can be on my own, I'll move in. Maybe in a day or so."

The time couldn't pass quickly enough for Elisabeth. She wanted to send this man on his way and get back to her normal routine.

* * *

Two days later, Gabe stood at the open window, staring out at the mountainside behind the Hart home. The day was bright and the scent of pine lay heavily on the air. He squinted at the forested foothills that rose above the grouping of houses. From half a dozen clotheslines, laundry flapped under the sun.

"You must be restless by now."

He turned at the male voice to see Sam Hart just inside the doorway. "You could say that, yes, sir," he replied.

"Did Elisabeth mention we're having guests for dinner this evening?"

He shook his head. Elisabeth didn't speak to him any more than was necessary.

"Think you're up to joining us? I'm sure you need a different perspective."

"Don't want to horn in on your company."

"Nonsense. You're a new citizen to Jackson Springs. It's time you meet a few townsfolk and let them get to know you. My wife and I enjoy having additional guests at our table."

Gabe nodded. "All right, then."

That evening Phillip showed up to assist him in dressing, though Gabe was able to prepare on his own. The lad talked nonstop, telling Gabe about a litter of kittens born under their back porch and how he'd been taking scraps to the mother cat.

Gabe handled the stairs more easily than the last time he'd attempted the descent, and Phillip directed him to the sitting room.

Sam stood from where he'd been sitting on a sofa beside a matronly woman and greeted them. He thanked Phillip and made the introductions.

The stout woman offered her hand in greeting and he touched her fingers briefly, ruefully remembering how he'd asked Elisabeth if their guest was a pretty widow woman. "Mrs. Jackson."

Getting to his feet, her son gave Gabe the once-over. His brown hair had been cut short and oiled into order with a precise part just shy of the center of his head. The lines from the teeth of his comb were visible. He wore shiny brown boots with a pinstriped brown suit. Not a bad-looking fellow. He extended a hand.

It came as no surprise to Gabe that Rhys Jackson didn't have any calluses on his palms. "Any connection to the town of Jackson Springs?" he asked.

"My father's father founded this town thirty-six years ago," Rhys answered.

He wasn't overly tall, but he was built sturdily, with wide shoulders and a broad chest. "Where are you from?" Rhys asked.

"Born in Illinois but traveled of late."

"What's your trade?" he asked.

"Worked in a machine shop for a spell," he replied. "I've made shingles and built bridges. Even mined salt for a time."

"Couldn't make up your mind?" Rhys asked.

Gabe picked up on the barb. "Like to keep my options open."

One of Elisabeth's sisters was seated on a bench near a window, and she studied Gabe curiously.

Sam glanced at her. "Have you met Anna?"

"I haven't."

"Anna is my youngest daughter—at least for the time being. Anna, meet Mr. Taggart."

"I'm pleased to make your acquaintance, sir," she said and rose to greet him with a little bow and a bashful nod.

"Your daughters are equally lovely," Gabe said to his host.

Anna's hair was paler than Elisabeth's, not as dense or wavy however, and her smile was warm and infectious. He guessed her to be about sixteen. She held a closed book, her index finger keeping her spot. Once the attention was turned away from her, she opened the book and apparently picked up where she'd left off. She seemed content and confident. Watching her made him think about his sister and wonder about the years of her childhood and youth, growing up at the academy and not with a family like this one. He'd never had experience with this kind of atmosphere before.

He'd always believed he'd made the best choice for her, and he still did.

He couldn't have provided her education or safe upbringing if he'd had to work in a mine or a factory. The few times he visited the school, he'd been impressed by the stability and routine. Irene had been given every opportunity that an education and a respectable background could provide.

Now she needed a husband with a good job and a secure future. Someone established and responsible.

He glanced at Rhys. At a break in the conversation, he asked, "What do you do, Mr. Jackson?"

"After his death, I took over my father's position as president of Rocky Mountain Savings and Trust."

"Banking," Gabe acknowledged with a nod.

Another fair-haired young lady came to announce it was time to take their places in the dining room, and he was introduced to Abigail.

"I've heard all about you from my little brothers," she told him with a twinkle in her eye. "Of course their descriptions are exciting and involve guns and robbers."

She was younger than Elisabeth, not quite as slender, but just as pretty. He had to wonder if Elisabeth would shine in the same way if she allowed herself a charming smile and the same exuberance.

They reached an enormous dining room with a long table suited to dinners such as this. The table itself had a covering made of fancy needlework, and atop it were platters and bowls holding a mound of mashed potatoes, mouthwatering sliced beef, a slaw and other vegetables. He'd never seen so much food outside a restaurant in his life.

Rhys seated his mother and took the chair beside her as though familiar with the arrangement. Gabe waited for instruction.

"Please, sit here," Josie said, standing behind an empty chair.

"Thank you, ma'am." He stood behind the chair she indicated, but waited until she sat to take his own seat.

Sam sat at the head of the table, his wife at his right

and Mrs. Jackson on his left, putting Rhys directly across from Gabe. Josie was on Gabe's right.

Sam continued with introductions, and Gabe learned the twin to his left was John. Beside John sat their nanny, Miss Tyler, and then Peter. Phillip sat at the foot of the table, and along the other side were Abigail, Anna and beside Rhys, Elisabeth.

As the food was passed and he helped himself, he considered the seating arrangement. Were Elisabeth and Rhys courting? He couldn't picture her accompanying him for a buggy ride or a picnic, but then maybe it was only Gabe she behaved so poorly toward. He made a point to pay close attention to her interaction with the others.

She chatted with Anna on her right, and Anna told her about a dress one of her classmates had worn that day. Elisabeth lent her undivided attention to the description.

"We might want to spend a few days in Denver," Elisabeth suggested. "That shop where we found the periwinkle gabardine might have a similar lace."

She appeared sincerely interested in helping her sister create a dress like her friend's.

There was a loud rasp, like the turn of a doorbell, and Elisabeth stood, holding out her hand as though to stop Josie from standing. She dropped her napkin on the seat of her chair, reminding him he hadn't even unfolded his. "I'll get it," she said.

Gabe opened his napkin discreetly.

"Where are you from?" Josie asked from beside him.

"Born in Illinois," he replied.

"I'm from Nebraska. Sam found me there and brought me to Colorado."

"A divine appointment to be sure," Sam said with a fond smile directed at his wife.

Elisabeth returned. "It's a telegram for Mr. Taggart." She handed him the folded and sealed paper and went back to her seat.

Uncertain what to expect, Gabe opened the telegram. His examination shot directly to the sender. Irene Taggart.

Tired of waiting STOP Will arrive on the tenth STOP Cannot wait to see you STOP.

His food rested uncomfortably in his belly. He hadn't told his sister he'd been shot. The last time he'd contacted her he'd told her his arrival date in Jackson Springs and assured her he'd send for her when he had a home ready.

He didn't have a home ready.

"Bad news?" Sam asked, and Gabe realized everyone's attention had focused on him and the piece of paper he held.

"No. No, it's good news, actually." He folded the telegram and tucked it into his shirt pocket. "My sister will be arriving sooner than I'd expected."

"You have a *sister?*" Elisabeth asked, the first time she'd spoken to him since he'd entered the dining room.

"Is that so hard to believe?"

Sam looked at his daughter, and she attempted to

cover her surprise. "I just never pictured you with a family."

"I wasn't hatched."

An uncomfortable silence settled on the gathering until Josie interrupted it with, "Do you have family other than your sister?"

"My folks died a long time ago," he answered. "Irene's been at boarding school in Chicago."

"How old is she?" Anna asked.

He thought a second. "Must be she's nineteen now."

The news that Gabe Taggart had a sister shouldn't have surprised Elisabeth, but it did. People weren't born in a vacuum, but if she'd been going to imagine his family, she'd have thought up scruffy-bearded brothers, not a sister at a boarding school.

"I own land nearby," he said, as though offering an explanation to the others. "I'd planned to have looked it over by now and started building a house, so I'm behind."

Rhys focused his attention on the other man. "Where is this land of yours?"

"From what I can tell, the piece is northwest of here," Gabe replied, then shrugged. "Doc won't let me ride, so I haven't seen it."

"Do you think you could tolerate a buggy ride?" Sam asked. "We could go look at it tomorrow."

Gabe smiled, his teeth white. "I'd be obliged, Reverend."

"Your sister is welcome to stay here with us," Josie offered.

Elisabeth couldn't quite pinpoint the look that crossed

his features. He studied Josie for a moment before speaking. "That's generous of you, ma'am, but I've got a place for us to stay until I build a house."

"Oh, really?" Beatrice entered the conversation for the first time. "And where will that be?"

"Seems it's nearby from what Elisabeth tells me." He tore his gaze from Josie to glance at the older woman.

"The parsonage," Elisabeth explained. "Mr. Taggart has rented it."

"Well, that is close by," Josie said. "You'll be able to join us for dinner at least once a week, and I won't hear any different."

"I can't argue with an invitation like that." The smile he gave Elisabeth's stepmother softened his features. His green eyes actually sparkled with appreciation. Elisabeth experienced an odd feeling, like the falling sensation in a dream, and placed both hands on the tabletop to steady herself.

"This is the best meal I've eaten in months," Gabe said. "The Hart females sure know their way around a kitchen."

"I made rice pudding," Abigail added, quickly vying for his attention.

He raised his eyebrows in surprise and appreciation.

"It's still warm." Abigail glanced at her stepmother. "May I serve it now?"

"Just as soon as we clear away a few dishes," Josie replied.

Elisabeth slid out her chair with the backs of her

knees and stood. "Abigail and I will clear the dishes. You stay seated."

Kalli got up. "I'll help."

In the kitchen, Abigail said to Kalli, "Mr. Taggart is handsome, don't you think?"

Kalli blushed. "Indeed," she agreed. "It's not fair that a man has eyelashes like that."

Elisabeth scraped plates and rinsed them in the pail in the sink before stacking them. Handsome? She supposed if he'd ever done anything but scowl at her, she'd have a different opinion of the man, but he hadn't smiled at her like he'd smiled at the others this evening. Not that she'd wanted him to. She'd never have imagined her stepmother and siblings to be so easily fooled.

On her next trip for more dishes, she deliberately looked at his eyelashes. He caught her stare, and she turned away in discomfit.

Abigail carried her bowl of steaming cinnamon-scented rice pudding to the table and Elisabeth placed a stack of painted china jelly dishes beside it. Abigail sat, so Elisabeth spooned pudding and carried the bowls around the table, placing them in front of the diners. When she reached Gabe, she stood as far away as possible and leaned in to set the dish before him.

He turned a curious glance upward. "Thank you."

"We don't need any bridges."

Elisabeth glanced up to discover Rhys speaking to Gabe.

"And there are no salt mines nearby. Will you be making shingles in Jackson Springs?"

She sensed a mocking edge, as though Rhys was

belittling the other man's skills or perhaps even questioning his intent.

"Actually, I'm planning to invest," Gabe replied.

Rhys lifted his eyebrows. "As in stocks?"

"Perhaps. But I'm more interested in finding someone who needs capital to get a business started. I don't want to work the business, so as long as it's a sound principle. I'd be a silent partner. Meanwhile I'll buy a few horses and try my hand at ranching."

Gabe had Rhys's attention now. The man sat forward, ignoring the dessert placed before him to focus on Gabe. "And you have the capital to fund a venture such as that?"

It was a rude question, akin to asking the man how much money he had, but Rhys was a banker, and she supposed it was his nature to question.

"That I do, Mr. Jackson."

"Rhys. Call me Rhys."

Chapter Six

Elisabeth set down the last dish in front of Abigail with a thud. Well, if that didn't beat all. Her father had taken the man in, and between him and Josie they'd made certain Elisabeth saw to all his needs. Her little brothers thought he was a hero, Abigail and Kalli called him handsome, and now even Rhys had rallied around Gabe's camp because Gabe had money to put in his bank. None of them had seen his antagonistic side or experienced his cutting tone.

He never had a civil word to say to her, but he was all smiles and compliments around everyone else.

"I've never tasted rice pudding this good," he told Abigail, and she blushed to the pale blond roots of her hair. "In fact I don't know when I've ever eaten so well. Reverend, your wife and daughters are excellent cooks."

"That they are," Sam replied with a proud grin.

Elisabeth rolled her eyes. Abigail noted it and frowned at her.

A knock sounded at the door, and this time Sam raised a hand to the others. "I'll get this one."

When he returned, he gave his wife's shoulder an apologetic squeeze. "I'm needed at the Quinn place. Seems Ezra collapsed and the doc thinks it's his heart."

"Oh, my," Josie said. "Well, we'll pray for him right now. You hurry on."

"Girls, you look after Josie tonight," Sam said with a look at Abigail and Anna. And then he turned to Elisabeth. "I never know how these types of things will go, so if I shouldn't get back in time, Elisabeth, please take our guest to see his land tomorrow. Take Phillip along if you need another hand."

Her heart sank, but she nodded obediently. "Yes, sir."

As soon as Sam was gone, Josie reached across the table for Beatrice's hand and Gabe's on her left. She closed her eyes.

Gabe hadn't held a woman's hand in a good long time, and never while the woman prayed, so Josie's action caught him off guard. Decidedly uncomfortable, he waited to see what happened next.

"Elisabeth, please pray for Mr. Quinn," she said, surprising him even more.

But Elisabeth didn't hesitate. "Father God, we lift our friend Ezra Quinn to You and ask that You would touch him with Your healing hand. We believe Your Word that says Jesus took our infirmities and bore our sicknesses, so we thank You that Mr. Quinn is delivered and whole this night in Jesus's name."

"And we pray for Ezra's boy, Lester," Josie added.

"Give him strength and comfort and provide for him from Your gracious bounty. Thank You, Lord," Josie said and the others chorused their amens before she released Gabe's hand.

Gabe didn't set much store by their faith, and he sure didn't think any prayer was going to make a difference if the man had already had a heart attack and his number was up.

They finished their dessert without their former enthusiasm, and Elisabeth and her sisters cleaned up the table. Josie ushered Sam and the Jacksons into a large sitting room. Sam's ribs ached something fierce, but he remained seated on an overstuffed chair until Elisabeth finished her chores and joined them.

"Excuse me," he said to the others. "I'm going to go upstairs and lie down."

Beatrice and Rhys said their goodbyes, and he climbed the stairs, Elisabeth on his heels.

"Would you like your medicine?" she asked.

He shook his head. "I'll just lie down."

"Suit yourself."

"You don't have to take me anywhere tomorrow. I'm sure I can find a driver and a buggy."

"If my father doesn't return, I'll accompany you," she assured him. She lit the lamp on the bureau and turned down the covers on the bed. Picking up the empty pitcher, she headed for the door. "I'll bring fresh water as soon as I've heated more."

"Much obliged," he said with a nod. Once she was gone, he eased onto the bed and closed his eyes. He didn't like being indisposed, and he really didn't like being indebted to the ungracious Elisabeth Hart. Even if she did have the prettiest eyes this side of the Rio Grande. It had been plain from the start that she didn't want any part of him and was only seeing to his needs out of obedience to her father.

The sooner Gabe Taggart was out of here and on his own, the better.

He woke to the sounds of the family the following morning, shaved and dressed on his own, then found his way downstairs to the dining room where they'd eaten the night before.

The boys, seated in their same places, glanced up when he joined them. Anna sat on the other side of the table, but Abigail was missing.

"Is your ribs better?" Phillip asked.

"They must be," he replied. "But if this is better, I don't know how I got through the past couple of days."

"Grunting," Phillip replied with a serious nod.

"Guess I did my share of grunting," he agreed with a sheepish grin.

The twins giggled.

Elisabeth hesitated in the doorway, then hurried forward and set down the bowl she'd been carrying. "Good morning, Mr. Taggart."

Obviously a greeting for the children's sake, because she didn't normally speak to him like that. "Good morning, Miss Hart. Has your father returned?"

"He came home for a few hours while it was still dark, but headed back to the Quinns'." She served her young brothers cooked oats and drizzled maple syrup on top of each one's bowl. "I will be accompanying you this morning. Phillip will join us."

"I will?" the lad asked with a hopeful expression. "And not go to school?"

"That's right." She stroked his back through his overalls and shirt. "I suppose we should pack a lunch in case we're out at noon."

He looked up at her with twinkling eyes. "Can I help?"

"Of course you can."

"I wanna go, too!" Peter announced. He already wore a glob of oatmeal on his shirtfront.

"Me, too," chirped John. At least Gabe thought that was John. The two younger boys looked just alike, but if they were sitting on the same chairs as last night, he had them straight.

Their mother entered the room carrying a platter of buttered toasted bread in time to hear their pleas.

"You're staying with Mama this morning," she said and gave each of them a kiss on the forehead and wiped Peter's shirt with a damp towel. "I need your help kneading bread."

John held up a bent arm to show her his biceps muscle. "I can hewp you, Mama. I gots big muscles. See?"

Abigail joined them, breathlessly seating herself, taking a piece of toasted bread and spreading jam on it. "Are you ready, Anna?"

"I've been ready. You're the one who changed clothing three times." She stood and picked up a stack of books and a lunch pail from the sideboard before giving Josie a peck on the cheek. "Where's Kalli?"

"Hanging wash out back. Don't fret about me. Have a good day at school."

After the girls hurried out, Elisabeth sat and ate.

The routine and the scurrying were foreign to Gabe. He'd eaten alone and traveled by himself most of his life, sleeping in his bedroll under the stars or in stark hotel rooms. Hotel dining rooms served decent meals, but most of the time he bought food in cafes or saloons and on the trail ate whatever he could carry with him.

He sure wasn't used to females or the order and stability they created by their very natures. The Hart daughters were training to be wives and mothers like the one who'd just seated herself beside him. And now... he could even picture Elisabeth as a wife. She was efficient and hardworking, and she had a different side to her when she interacted with her family. Nurturing... loving.

The discovery was unexpected. And unwelcome.

Apparently he was the only one who brought out her defensiveness and sarcasm.

"Enjoy your ride," Josie said, once she'd finished eating. "Elisabeth, I prepared chopped chicken, and you're welcome to make sandwiches for your lunch. Phillip, I want to hear that you were on your best behavior today."

He hopped down from his chair and ran to give her an uninhibited hug. "Yes'm. I'll be Lis'beth's helper."

"Shall I go get a buggy and bring it up the hill?"

Elisabeth was looking at Gabe. "Or do you think you can walk to the livery with me?"

He wouldn't admit in a hundred years that her bringing the buggy to him sounded like a good idea, so he assured her he could walk just fine.

Once everything was prepared, the three of them exited the house, and Gabe had his first real look at the neighborhood. The Harts' home sat at the top of a steep incline, nestled against the forested mountainside. The closest homes were farther down the hill, but none was as impressive as the three-storied beauty on the hill.

"That's the parsonage you've rented." At the bottom of the street, Elisabeth pointed out a tiny square white house that sat beside the church with only a lot separating the two.

"That's *it?*" he asked.

"If you recall, you never mentioned your sister to me," she explained. "And I did ask if you wanted to see it first," she added. "Since you neglected to tell me about your sister, I assumed you would be the only one living there. Two people can manage just fine, though. There are two small bedrooms."

"I didn't know she was coming so soon," he said. "I hoped to have a house built before she got here."

"You know what they say about the plans of men," she said.

"No. Who said something about plans?"

She glanced at him. "Well, there are proverbs about the plans of men."

"Chinese proverbs?"

Her next glance indicated she questioned his sincerity. "The *book* of Proverbs, Mr. Taggart. It's in the Bible."

"I've heard of it. So what does it say?"

"Well…there's one that says a man's heart devises his way, but the Lord directs his steps."

"What does that mean?"

"I think it means that we can plan the way we want to live and the things we want to do, but only God can enable us to live it and do those things."

"Did that Confucius fellow write that?"

"No, Solomon wrote it."

"Is Solomon his first or last name?"

She turned to discover him studying her from beneath the brim of his hat. His attention was flattering in a way she didn't want to admit, but she suspected he was enjoying himself too much at her expense. "*King* Solomon, the father of David who wrote most of the Psalms. Solomon was the wisest man who ever lived."

"Hmm. Suppose he ever took a day off from being so smart?"

He was baiting her, and she wasn't going to fall into another of his antagonistic traps. "If he had, he wouldn't have been near as wise, now would he?" She struggled to remember the initial subject. "The house is small, yes. But you'll manage just fine."

Phillip had brought along his harmonica, and from behind them came discordant sounds as he did his six-year-old's rendition of "Shoo Fly Don't Bother Me," stopping and starting to get the notes right.

Elisabeth couldn't resist a smile. Her brother's playing ended their conversation, which was just fine with her.

She followed Warren Burke's directions, which he'd given at the time they'd rented the buggy, and left the road to head across an open meadow. They neared a stream and she guided the horses to a stop.

Gabe pointed to a shallow section where rocks protruded above the water. "We can cross over there."

"I can't take the buggy across this water."

"It's just a little stream. Barely two feet deep right here."

She didn't have the same paralyzing fear that her younger sister Anna did, but all the same, Elisabeth didn't like crossing water. Just seeing the sun reflecting from the surface and glimpsing the small fish darting in a hollow against the bank made her heart thud against her breastbone.

It had been over seven years, but the memory of the day their wagon had tipped over in a rushing river was as fresh as if it had been only the day before. The water had been startlingly cold, sucking away her breath. Immediately her sodden skirts had made treading water impossible, and she'd swiftly been carried downstream. Miraculously, she'd spotted a branch protruding over the water and grabbed for it successfully.

The branch had been solid and she'd had a death grip. Most likely she could have clung to it and survived even if her father had gone after her mother first. But Elisabeth's terrified screams had led him to her. She'd latched her arms around his neck and clung for dear life as he carried her up the bank to safety.

And then he'd left her beside her sisters and in the care of the other women of the wagon train to continue his search for her mother. The hunt had concluded with a devastating discovery.

"Here. Let me." Gabe took the reins from her fingers.

She released her hold, glad for the interruption of her thoughts.

He spoke softly to the horse, directing it down the gentle slope toward the water and encouraged it to proceed across the stream.

"Hold on!" Elisabeth called to her brother, then gripped the edge of the seat and didn't breathe while the buggy bounced over the rocky streambed and up the other side of the bank.

"That was fun!" Phillip shouted, leaning forward between them. "Can we do it again?"

"On the way back," Gabe replied.

Elisabeth released her pent-up breath and turned to gape at the man beside her. Wearing that irritatingly cocky grin, he dropped his gaze to her hand where she gripped his forearm.

It took her a full thirty seconds to distinguish the hard sinew beneath the fabric and release her hold. Embarrassment got a hold on her. She looked away.

Uncomfortably aware of the man beside her, she concentrated on the landscape. The horse pulled the buggy up a slope until they sat perched on the grassy rim above a meadow. A startled antelope fled into the aspens growing along the opposite hillside.

"Did you see that deer?" Phillip asked, excitement lacing his voice.

"That was a pronghorn antelope," Gabe told him. "A female."

The sky appeared incredibly pale against the vibrant greens of the trees and the rocky slopes glittering in the distance.

Still holding the reins, Gabe led the horse forward and halted near a patch of graceful blue columbines. "Let's stretch our legs."

Gingerly, he eased to the ground, and then reached back for Elisabeth. While she took her time wondering how she could avoid touching him, Phillip wedged around her and jumped to the ground with a whoop. He picked up a dried buffalo pile and sent it sailing through the air. Seconds later, he was running through grass up to his knees, startling half a dozen grouse that took wing.

"You stay close by!" Elisabeth called. Begrudgingly she accepted Gabe's help. His hand was warm and strong, and she released it as soon as her feet touched the ground.

Gabe set off at a quick pace, his long legs covering ground until he climbed a rise and stood silhouetted against the sky. Phillip spotted him and ran to join him. Elisabeth took a more sedate stroll, skimming her fingertips across the delicate petals of the wildflowers. It had been too long since she'd taken time to enjoy nature's beauty or the summer air. It seemed she was always too occupied with work to set aside an afternoon for a ride.

The sun beat down from a cloudless sky, warming her arms and shoulders through her cotton blouse, and she was glad for her straw hat. On a current of air, an eagle soared high above the timberline, dipping toward the trees, then disappearing.

Phillip looked tiny in the distance, appearing even smaller beside the broad-shouldered man. Gabe reached out and ruffled the boy's hair, and she could imagine the stream of questions spilling from her little brother.

Gabe left him and walked toward her, his outline growing larger as he neared.

Notes from Phillip's harmonica reached her on the hot breeze. She smiled to herself.

Gabe removed his hat, threaded his fingers through his hair and replaced it. He was an imposing sight, square-jawed and lean, that ever-present weapon strapped to his side. "You packed us a lunch, did you?"

She blinked to orient herself. "Yes."

She walked back to the buggy and reached behind the seat for the covered basket and the quilt. "How are your ribs feeling?"

"Not perfect," he replied. "But I've had a lot worse days."

She found a place where the grass had been flattened by wind or rain and deftly spread the faded quilt, then set the basket on it. It took only a minute to set out the food and napkins. "Phillip!"

He was still playing his harmonica, turning in a circle as he did so.

A breeze caught the edge of the quilt as Gabe lowered himself to a sitting position, and they both reached for the edge at the same time. Her hand lay on the back of his longer than necessary, but instead of pulling away, she stared in fascination at her slender white fingers against his long tanned ones.

He turned his hand over, palm up, until he held her hand, and still she didn't move away. Her heart picked up a staccato beat that surprised her even more than the touch.

With his other hand, he reached to tug off her hat.

She looked up at him then.

Even shaded beneath the brim of his hat, his eyes were as green as she remembered, reminding her of the first time she'd seen them—and him—that day on the train.

"In the sun your hair shines like spun gold," he said, surveying her hair and face with glittering green eyes.

He was so close she could smell the pressed cotton of his shirt.

"It's not as pretty as Abigail's," she said. "Hers curls on the ends and has reddish streaks."

"Yours is by far the prettiest," he disagreed. "Prettiest I've ever seen." It was the nicest—and most confusing—thing he'd ever said to her.

Her gaze dropped unerringly to his lips, conjuring up the memory of him talking to Phillip about kissing girls.

"Wonderin' if it tickles, are you?"

He was outrageously bold and improper, and she should have straightened and immediately taken back her hand...but she didn't. Because that was *exactly* what she'd been wondering.

One side of his mouth inched up, and the mocking familiarity sat with her more easily than his uncharacteristic compliment.

She couldn't have changed what happened next if she'd seen it coming.

And she should have seen it coming.

Chapter Seven

But when Gabe leaned ever-so-slightly forward, she ignored the warning of her erratic heartbeat and did the same. Their lips met. This was no Zebediah Turner kiss.

She wasn't thinking about the sun overhead or the off-key notes of the harmonica or the jar of pickles waiting to be opened. She was thinking about Gabe Taggart's warm mouth against hers.

Her father always said courting was a prelude to marriage. Kissing was part of courting, but she had no intention of marrying this man. She shouldn't be kissing him. She took her sweet time calling a halt to the experience, however. She was, in fact, foolishly reluctant to miss any part of it.

Nobody had ever called her hair spun gold before. No one had ever made her heart flutter as though hundreds of butterflies fought to get out of her chest. It was shallow to succumb to his flattery, but with him she felt different. Not quite herself…someone infinitely more exciting and attractive than plain old Elisabeth, the preacher's daughter.

She'd done nothing besides butt heads with this man since the first moment they'd met. She shouldn't find kissing him enjoyable. Elisabeth should have been offended…at the very least put off. The wisest and most prudent action called for moving away and putting an end to this appalling lapse in judgment while she still held a scrap of dignity intact.

"Look, Lis'beth! I ain't never seen a butterfly that color b'fore. What do you suppose it's called?"

Nudged back to her senses, Elisabeth straightened and withdrew her hand in one swift motion. Cheeks burning, she refused to raise her gaze, but reached for the wrapped sandwiches and purposefully kept the breathlessness from her voice to ask, "What color is it?"

Phillip dropped to his knees on the quilt, but thankfully his attention remained focused on the grassy meadow. "Black mostly, with white stripes and little white spots. See?"

She picked up her hat, plopped it back on her head and then peered in the direction he indicated. "I don't know much about butterflies."

"How 'bout you, Mr. Taggart?" the boy asked. "Do you know 'bout butterflies?"

"'Fraid not," he replied.

"We can get a picture book at the library, though," Elisabeth told her brother.

Phillip sat cross-legged and bit into a chicken-salad sandwich. "Did Mama make these?"

"Yes, she did."

Gabe picked up his sandwich. Out of habit, he pored over the meadow and surrounding tree line. Reassured that the three of them were alone, he unwrapped it and took a bite. Elisabeth's cheeks were still pink. Could be from the warmth of the sun, but he suspected the high color was more than that.

Kissing her caught him as unaware as he supposed it had had her. What foolishness was that? He hadn't come to Colorado looking for a woman. He already had Irene to look out for, and he didn't have the first idea how.

"Is your mama a good cook?" Phillip asked, snagging his attention.

"My mother's been gone a long time."

With a bread crumb on his chin, Phillip frowned. "Where'd she go?"

Not wanting to traumatize the lad, Gabe swung a questioning glance at Elisabeth. The Hart children seemed quite sheltered.

"Mr. Taggart means his mother is in heaven," she supplied.

Realization crossed the boy's features. "Ohh." He set down a triangular-shaped crust. "Lis'beth's first mama is in heaven, too. Isn't that so, Lis'beth?"

She nodded.

Phillip raised his eyebrows as an idea struck him. "Maybe they know each other!"

"Quite possibly," Elisabeth replied.

"An' Jesus is with 'em, isn't that right?"

She nodded. "That's right."

Gabe didn't hold much store by the whole idea of

heaven. He said nothing, but Elisabeth finally raised her gaze to him as though guessing his skeptical thoughts.

"You do believe in heaven, don't you?" she asked.

He didn't want to have this discussion with her, but he shrugged. "I think people make up their own beliefs to get them through grief—or to justify their behavior. Likely it feels better to think their loved ones are in a good place."

Her expression showed her shock. "Jesus said He was going ahead to the Father to prepare a place for us."

"Don't know anything about that," he replied. "Your mama makes good chicken salad, Phillip."

She was quiet the rest of the meal, and once they'd finished and she packed away the lunch items, Gabe stood and studied the land again. "Looks like a good spot for a house just over there." He pointed. "I could clear a few of those trees and leave the rest to shade the yard. Barn and corrals off that way."

"Will there be horses?" Phillip asked.

"Fine horses. And a few cows."

"What about chickens? Jimmy Fuller gots chickens at his place and he has to give 'em food and water every day. They make their own eggs!"

Gabe grinned. "A few chickens might be called for. Eggs make a fine breakfast."

"Maybe I can come help you sometimes. I'm gettin' bigger."

"That would be a fine idea, as long as your ma and pa say it's okay."

On the ride back, Phillip leaned against Elisabeth's

side and slept. The house at the top of the hill was uncommonly silent when they arrived.

Gabe followed Elisabeth inside, Phillip at her side. She removed her hat and hung it on one of the pegs that lined the exterior foyer wall. He followed her example.

The twins sat at the top of the stairs, quietly playing with wooden horses.

With one hand on the banister, Elisabeth climbed the steps. "Where's Mama?"

"In her room," John answered. "Westing."

With a swish of skirts, she hurried past them and disappeared along the upper hallway.

Gabe perched on a lower stair and watched the boys. He'd never seen them so silent.

Within a few minutes, Elisabeth returned. "Are you feeling well enough to fetch Dr. Barnes?"

He straightened with a nod. "What's wrong?"

"Everything's fine," she replied in a calm tone. "We're just going to have a new brother or sister very soon."

He glanced at the twins, then back at her. "Where's your father?"

"He hasn't yet returned from the Quinns."

"Do you suppose the doctor is still out there, too?"

"I have no idea."

"Better tell me where their place is, just in case."

"You can take the buggy," she offered.

"I'll return the buggy and get a horse."

"Are you able to ride?"

Without a reply, he loped down the stairs and grabbed his hat. "Take care of your mama. I'll be back."

He was relieved to have a task. Glad to be away from the unknown and uncomfortable atmosphere of child birthing.

When Warren Burke heard the news about Mrs. Hart, the liveryman loaned Gabe one of his own horses. The sleek speckled mare was some sort of Russian trotter mixed with Arabian blood. The white spots on its dark gray flanks resembled stars.

The horse had a black forelock and a gray tail that faded to lighter hair on the tips. Gabe took a liking to the unusually colored animal right off.

His side already ached from the day's exertion, but he pushed past the discomfort to focus on the job that needed doing. He checked the doc's house first. Matthew Barnes's wife told him her husband was right there at home, sleeping after his long night's vigil.

"I'll wake him and send him over to the Harts'," she assured Gabe.

Relieved, Gabe rode out of town. The Quinn farm was about a half hour ride. According to the landmarks, it was set to the west of Gabe's land, so it was probable his land adjoined the Quinn property. Studying the terrain again, he thought of all the years of travel, all the nights in a bedroll under the stars and those spent in a hotel room. Those hard years had paid for a future, and he was finally going to get to enjoy it.

Ezra Quinn's golden wheat fields waved under the afternoon sun. Gabe was no farmer, but it looked to him that it wouldn't be long before the wheat needed harvesting.

He'd grow hay to feed his horses and dig a well so Irene didn't have to go far for water. He was looking forward to getting to know his sister, but it was likely she wouldn't be with him that long. He would find her a good husband and see that she was settled and happy.

He spotted smoke curling from a chimney. A young man met him as he rode close to a one-story house and dismounted, holding his side. "Never seen you before, mister."

The young man was in his twenties, dressed in plain dungarees and a cotton shirt.

"Gabe Taggart. I'm lookin' for Samuel Hart."

"You the fella who shot those train robbers?"

Gabe nodded. "Is the preacher here?"

"In the house." The back door complained with a loud squeak as he led Gabe into a kitchen humid from an iron kettle steaming on the stove. "Back here. I'm Lester Quinn."

"Pleasure." Gabe snatched off his hat and worked to silence his boot heels on the wooden floor of the hallway beyond the kitchen.

Lester motioned for him to enter a dim room off to the left. Sam and a woman sat on chairs on opposite sides of a bed that held a motionless bald man.

Sam looked up, and it took a moment for recognition to dawn in his face. "Mr. Taggart?"

"Your wife's having the baby soon," Gabe told him.

Gabe glanced at the sleeping man in the bed.

"You go on home to your wife, Reverend," the woman said. "There's nothing more we can do here. I figure if God hasn't heard our prayers by now, He's not going to."

"He's heard them, Nell," Sam assured her. He followed Gabe outside, where the young man had anticipated his departure and hitched Sam's horse and buggy.

"Thank you, Reverend," Lester said. "You bein' here helped my mama a lot."

"That's why I'm here," Sam told him. "You see to it your mother gets some rest now. Maybe once I'm gone, she'll lie down."

"Yes, sir, Reverend."

Gabe rode a generous distance ahead of Sam so the horse wouldn't kick up dirt in his face, and they held a hasty pace. Thoughts of that brown bottle of medicine and the tranquil sleep it could bring taunted him. Doc Barnes had advised him not to ride, but he'd been all-fired convinced a lazy trip would do him well. He hadn't planned on extended hours in the saddle, however. While the animal beneath him had a sure, easy gallop, regardless Gabe's cracked rib had weathered a beating.

The hill to the house was the longest stretch of the trip. At last the sight of the gabled and turreted home relieved his tension. He eased the horse to a halt and dismounted to take the buggy reins from Sam. "I'll return the rig," he told him. "You go on."

With a distracted thank-you, Sam hurried up the steep brick stairs that led to the gate and the yard beyond.

Gabe routinely checked the ground and the area for anything out of the ordinary, then tied the horse to the back of the buggy and turned the rig to head down the hill. He'd pay the liveryman's helper to give him a ride back.

He reached Main Street just as a locomotive released steam from its engine a few blocks away. He checked the street in both directions and made his way toward the livery.

"Mr. Taggart!"

At the call, his instincts went on alert. He turned to discover a reed-thin young man waving at him from the front of the telegraph building. The fellow stepped out from the shade of the overhang into the sunlight, and Gabe flexed his fingers without tensing his body.

"I have a message for you."

Relieved at the harmless notice, Gabe relaxed and met him in the street.

"I been lookin' for you," the younger man said. "Your sister is waiting for you at Mrs. Rhodes's café. I told her I'd watch for you and give you her message."

"Did you say my sister is here?"

"Yes, sir, Mr. Taggart."

Confused, Gabe reached into his pocket for a coin and flipped it in the air. "Thanks."

"I'm Junie Pruitt, by the way. In case you should need any errands done. Deliver messages, carry supplies, anything like that. You can find me on Main Street in the morning, and later in the day you can pin notes on the wall at the barber shop. I check 'em regular like."

"Good to know." Looked like he wouldn't be taking the buggy back just yet. Gabe searched out the café.

Irene shouldn't have arrived for another couple weeks. How was he going to take care of her when he'd had someone taking care of him until now? He hadn't even looked at the house he'd rented, though Elisabeth had assured him it was clean.

Why hadn't he thought to ask Junie Pruitt to handle Irene's luggage? This was a fine kettle of fish.

He no more than made it through the doorway before a woman in a jade-green traveling suit stood from beside the table where she'd been seated. She wore a feathery little hat that matched her jacket. "Gabriel!"

Her hair was as dark as he remembered, near black like his, but the rest of her... She looked nothing like the little sister he remembered. The person who hurried toward him was a beautiful woman, a woman with curves in places little sisters didn't have curves. "Irene?"

She flung herself toward him and before he could protect himself, she had crushed herself against him in an exuberant hug. The pressure against his ribs took his breath away. He managed to hold back all but a grunt.

"What's this?" she asked, leaning back and peeling open his jacket. Her eyes widened at the sight of his revolver. "I've never seen so many guns in my life as on my trip west," she told him. "Seems everyone has a weapon." She gave him a curious glance. "Am I going to need a gun? A woman on the train showed me the pearl-handled derringer she carried in her unmentionables. It was quite attractive actually. I wouldn't mind one of those."

"I wasn't expecting you for two more weeks," he said.

"I was weary of staying at a hotel," she told him. "My welcome wore out at school. After graduation all the other girls my age left. I helped with the younger children, but I'm not really cut out for nursemaid duty." She pulled a face.

"Children take so much work, don't you know. They are always hungry or spilling something...and the babies? Well, we won't even go into that."

"Are your belongings at the station?"

"Yes. I paid a nice fellow to watch them for me while I came here to get out of the sun. I can't wait to bathe and change into fresh clothing. Is your place far?"

"Actually...I've been staying with the preacher's family. There was a mishap on the train the day I arrived, and I was injured."

"Gabriel!" she said, her eyes wide with concern. "Are you all right?"

"Fine. Couple of tender ribs is all. I do have a small place rented. We'll stay there temporarily while our house is built."

"You're building a house for us?"

He nodded and urged her toward the door. The few patrons in the café had been staring while they reunited.

"Where is it?"

"Not far from town, but the building hasn't started yet."

"We won't be living in town?"

"My land is to the southwest. Not far, I assure you. You can come to town whenever you like. Often."

"All right."

She didn't appear entirely convinced about the idea of living away from Jackson Springs. "You won't be cut off from friends or shops."

He guided her to the buggy and headed toward the station. "I was thinking more about wild animals and Indians," she said. "I've heard stories about the danger of leaving civilization behind."

"Any Indians out our way will be friendly."

"What about wolves and bears?"

"I've spent years on the trail, and I've never had a run-in with a bear."

"A wolf?"

"A time or two," he answered begrudgingly.

She gaped at him in obvious concern.

"Maybe I will teach you to use a rifle," he decided. It was better to teach her to use a gun safely and with confidence than to leave her unprotected. He would have work to do and couldn't watch her every minute.

At the station, Gabe paid the fellow watching Irene's trunks and valises to load them into the buggy. He supposed he could check the two of them into the hotel. Josie had generously offered that his sister could join him at the Harts', but now with the baby arriving today, he didn't want to add more work and additional complication to their lives.

Briefly, he explained that his hosts were in the middle of a family event. He stopped the buggy and gestured for Irene to climb the steep stairs ahead of him. At the top, he masked his grimace and fatigue to take her hand and lead her up the porch stairs and, with a tap on the door, into the house.

"Oh, there you are!"

He looked up in surprise to see Elisabeth and Abigail coming from the back hall. Elisabeth handed the covered tray she carried to Abigail, and the girl carried it up the stairs.

"How is Mrs. Hart?" he asked.

"She's just fine," Elisabeth answered. "And so is the baby."

"He came already?"

"She," she said with a smile. "Rachel." She turned to Irene with a questioning expression.

"This is my sister, Irene." He gestured to Elisabeth. "Elisabeth Hart."

"I had no idea you would be here so soon." Elisabeth surprised him by taking Irene's hand and offering her a warm smile. "Welcome to Jackson Springs and to our home. You must be exhausted."

"I am weary of the dust," his sister replied with a smile. "It's a pleasure to make your acquaintance, Mrs. Hart."

"Oh, no, just Miss, but you must call me Elisabeth. There are far too many Miss Harts around here to keep us all straight." She glanced at Gabe, then back. "We'll get your belongings carried up to a room for you. I'm guessing they're outside now? And meanwhile I'll run you a bath."

"I was gonna get my things and take Irene to a hotel,"

Gabe told her. "You folks have your plate full already without us adding to the workload."

"You know Josie would never allow that to happen," she replied. "You will both stay right here until we get you situated in the parsonage."

"The parsonage?" Irene asked.

"My father's the preacher," Elisabeth told her. "But when you see the house, you'll know why we never lived there. Not that it isn't clean or nice," she hastened to add. "Just that we're a big family, and the house is small."

Abigail came back downstairs at that moment, and Elisabeth made introductions. "My sister Abigail will show you back to the bathing chamber and get water for your bath while I see to having your things brought in."

Once the two young women were gone, Elisabeth turned to him. "You didn't tell her, did you?"

Chapter Eight

Only years of inflexible restraint kept him from revealing his panic at her question. What did she know? "What?"

"That you were shot."

His alarm subsided. "How did you know that?"

"Because you're standing there with pain written on every angle of your face, but she didn't show a fleck of concern. Had she known, she would've sent you to bed, like I'm doing right this minute."

He jerked a thumb over his shoulder toward the door. "But I—"

"No discussion. I'll see to the trunks and the buggy. Take the medicine on the bureau if you know what's good for you." She took his arm and guided him toward the stairs. "I'll settle your sister for a nap of her own, and you won't be missed."

Gabe took in her flushed face, the earnest concern in her blue eyes, and felt the warmth of her hand through his sleeve. Her tone and words were as brusque as ever. Yes, she was as sensible and practical as always, but for this moment genuine warmth was evidenced in her behavior as well, catching him more off guard than his sister's unexpected arrival.

His thoughts traveled unerringly to their kiss that afternoon. That had been a mistake. He'd intended to tease and see her reaction, be it disgust or shock, but he hadn't intended an honest-to-goodness kiss. Never in a thousand years had he expected her to lean in and kiss him back.

Even if he did have time or the inclination to take a wife in the future—and it for sure wouldn't be until after Irene was married off and his ranch was established—this woman with her talk of heaven and Jesus, along with her persnickety ways, wasn't suited to him.

His ribs hurt so bad he was sick to his stomach. He lent all his energy into making it up the stairs and to the bed without losing the contents of his stomach on her shoes.

He hated that she'd recognized his weakness. He wasn't accustomed to letting anyone see him less than strong and confident, but there was nothing he could do about it at the moment. He made it as far as the bed and half fell onto the quilt.

She reached for a boot and tugged it off, then the other. "Take off your gun," she ordered, and he complied. She took it from him, surprising him again, rolled the holster and tucked the gun and belt under his pillows. "Will you take the medicine?"

"Half a spoon," he conceded. She measured the dose and held it to his lips. He swallowed and collapsed back upon the pillows. "Thank you, Elisabeth."

"You're welcome." She slid the curtains shut, closing out the late afternoon sun.

He felt better already.

Before he was aware, she'd left the room, closing the door behind her.

Elisabeth and Abigail prepared and served a late supper. Their father took his seat, appearing weary, but joyful. He said a blessing over their meal, thanking God for the new life in their home and for Josie's recovery.

"Are you happy baby Rachel is a girl, Papa?" Phillip asked.

"I'm quite happy," Sam replied. "It was time we had another girl."

Kalli sliced ham for the twins and cut it into bite-size pieces. "She's sure a pretty little thing. I never knew babies were so tiny."

"You don't have any younger siblings?" Sam asked.

"No, Reverend," Kalli answered. I have two older brothers. The only babies I've seen are those at church, but they're so much bigger."

"You'll be surprised how quickly she will get bigger," Sam told her.

"Mr. Taggart's sister arrived this afternoon," Elisabeth said. "I've given her my room, so I'll be bunking with you until we get them settled down the street." She glanced at Anna.

"Isn't her arrival sooner than expected?" Sam asked.

Elisabeth explained with what little she knew.

"You did exactly what Josie would have," Sam told

her. "Of course Irene and Mr. Taggart are welcome here until they can move to the parsonage."

"Where is she?" Anna asked.

Elisabeth explained that Irene had been exhausted from her travels. "I'll prepare plates for both of them and keep their food warm."

"I am blessed that my daughters are capable cooks and gracious hostesses," their father said with a smile for each of them. "You will make fine wives for three lucky young men."

"I might not get married, Papa," Anna said.

Her father and siblings studied her curiously.

"I want to study, like you," she said earnestly. "I want to be like my namesake in the Bible and do great things for God."

Sam appeared thoughtful for a moment before he spoke. "I am confident that all my children will accomplish great things for God," he said kindly. "Whether they are married or not."

At his words, Anna smiled and picked up her glass of milk.

Elisabeth looked upon her younger sister with fond appreciation. She'd begun to wonder whether or not a husband was in her own future. If the disappointing selection of possible mates she'd seen so far was any indication, she doubted she'd become a wife anytime soon. No one could measure up to her father.

A bright bit of burnt orange caught her attention at the doorway, and Elisabeth glanced up to find Irene standing hesitantly at the entrance to the room.

"Come in!" Elisabeth stood to usher her toward an

empty chair. Picking up a plate and silverware from the extras on the sideboard, she set a place before her and handed her a napkin. "We've only just sat down."

Elisabeth made introductions. "Were you able to rest?"

"I had a pleasant nap, thank you. Where is my brother?"

"He's resting," she replied. "I'll keep a plate of food warm for him if he doesn't come down now."

Irene took the bowl of fried potatoes Kalli passed and helped herself. "Is it common for him to sleep through supper?"

"He must've worn himself out riding today," Sam supplied. "He's only just been getting around a couple of days."

Irene's eyes widened.

"Josie and Elisabeth nursed him back to health," he added. "And fed him well, which I'm sure helped him recover."

"What happened exactly?" she asked. "All I know is he has tender ribs, but he didn't explain."

"Mr. Taggart shot the bandits what was robbing Lis'beth and the other people on the train," Phillip piped up.

Elisabeth's heart sank. She hadn't had time to prepare the children, but what would she have said anyway? She couldn't have encouraged them not to tell the truth. But Gabe hadn't wanted to upset his sister.

"That's how he got shot," Phillip supplied.

Color drained from Irene's face, and she set down the

potato bowl with a thunk, sending her spoon flying, but unaware. "Shot? Gabriel was shot?"

"He's perfectly fine," Elisabeth assured her. "His rib deflected the bullet, but was cracked, so it's quite painful."

Irene stood, dropping her napkin beside her plate and abandoning her food before she'd taken a bite. "He said nothing."

"I'm sure he didn't want you to worry," Elisabeth replied.

The other young woman turned and left the dining room.

Not knowing whether or not to follow, Elisabeth looked at her father for guidance. She didn't want to intrude on their family moment, but perhaps she could act as a buffer between the siblings. She wasn't sure why she cared.

At her father's shrug, she got up and followed, hurrying up the stairs.

Hearing Elisabeth's steps behind her, Irene paused in the upstairs hallway. "Which room is he in?"

Elisabeth moved past her and led the way to a closed door. "This one. He might still be sleeping."

Irene glanced at her, and then turned the knob and pushed open the door. The room was still dim and Gabe lay motionless upon the bed. She moved forward, and the floorboard under her foot creaked.

At the same split second, Gabe shot into motion, reaching beneath a pillow to produce his revolver, and aiming it at Irene with a deadly click.

Chapter Nine

Elisabeth's heart stopped momentarily before hammering against her ribs at the thundering speed of a locomotive. Irene stifled a cry. Pressing both hands against her midriff, she stood on her toes as though the position elevated her from harm.

"Irene!" he barked. "Don't ever sneak up on a man like that." He tucked the gun away and moved to a sitting position.

"You scared ten years off my life," she told him. "Who did you think had come into your room?"

Elisabeth was now wondering the same thing.

He ran a hand over his eyes. "You took me unaware, is all."

"Well, I was unaware, too," she said with an accusatory tone. "You neglected to tell me you'd been in a gunfight and were *shot*."

He glanced at Elisabeth, and she shook her head to say it hadn't been her who told. "It wasn't precisely like that," he denied.

The incident had been *exactly* like that, but Elisabeth kept her mouth shut.

"You shot men who were robbing the train?" his sister asked.

"Not until the situation turned dangerous and lives were at stake. Then I did the only thing I could."

"And one of them shot you?"

"I wasn't quite fast enough."

Elisabeth studied him in the dimness. Hadn't been fast enough? He'd felled half a dozen men in the time it took her to draw a breath!

"What if you'd been killed?" Irene asked, her voice breaking. "What if I'd arrived in Jackson Springs to *that* news?" She raised a hand to her brow and stood like that, half shielding her eyes from view. "What would I have done without you?"

"It was my fault," Elisabeth said then, surprising herself and apparently Gabe, because he turned toward her with his black brows in the air.

Irene turned to face her.

"When those men held up the train and asked for all of our valuables…" She touched her fingers to the ring under her bodice. "I hesitated. I didn't mean to put anyone in danger. It was instinct, a protective reaction to the possibility of losing my mother's ring." She looked at Gabe. "He warned me to hand over my belongings so no one got hurt, but I dragged my feet too long. If I'd simply complied, the bandits would have taken their booty and left us in peace."

"You can't know that for sure," Gabe interjected.

"But you said—"

"At the time going along peacefully seemed the reasonable thing," he said. "We have no way of knowing if they'd have shot passengers or not. Thieves are an unpredictable lot."

Elisabeth blinked. This day had been full of surprises. His summation was the extreme opposite of anything he'd said regarding the holdup until now. He'd blamed her for all the injuries, including his own. She didn't know how to react to the pardon. But perhaps his understanding was only for his sister's sake. Elisabeth didn't care why he'd changed his tune. Irene was a gently raised young woman, who had traveled all this way to unite with her brother. Elisabeth understood firsthand what it was like to leave behind everything familiar and comfortable and face the uncertainty of starting over.

She also knew what losing a mother was like, though Irene had lost both her parents, and Elisabeth had always had her sisters for company and comfort. This girl had only Gabe.

She looked at him. May the good Lord help her. Sensing the tension between brother and sister, Elisabeth changed the subject. "Dinner is on the table right now. May I bring you a plate?"

"I'll come down." Getting to his feet without placing a hand against his side must have taken gumption, or he truly was much better. "Just give me a few minutes to wash up." Anticipating her next words, he said, "The water from this morning is just fine. I'll be down shortly."

Dismissed, she and Irene walked out, and Elisabeth closed the door behind her.

"You lost your mother?" Irene asked.

"Seven years ago," she answered.

Irene blinked. "But all those small children..."

"My father remarried. Josie is resting right now. A brand-new baby sister was born just today."

"And you've all been so gracious, when you already have a house—and your hands—full."

"Josie loves it that way. She was the one who initially suggested you stay with us."

"I shall look forward to meeting her."

"You won't be disappointed." She walked ahead of Elisabeth to the top of the stairs. "I lost both of my parents at the same time. Gabriel saw to my care and education. I've been counting the days until I could leave boarding school. I can't wait to live in a real home and get to know my brother."

"I can attest that it's his priority to make a home for you. Having his plans thwarted did not rest well."

They returned to the dining room, where Gabe joined them within a few minutes. He sat next to his sister, and she looked over at him with adoration.

Sam inquired about Abigail's and Anna's day at school, and once they'd finished sharing the details of their day—before they'd been summoned home to meet their new sister—he asked the twins what they'd done. Kalli filled in missing details. Finally he glanced at Elisabeth, then over at Gabe. "And how was your ride? How does the land appear?"

"Fertile," Gabe replied. "There are trees and bushes

everywhere, so there's underground water. We saw streams. Of course I haven't looked over all of the property, but it doesn't appear anyone's ever settled there, and if they have it's been in years past. There are meadows for hay and grassland for pastures. And a flat spot for a house and stables and corrals."

"If you grow grapes, they will have to be carried on a stick between two men," Elisabeth joked.

Gabe looked at her like she'd spoken another language. "That's absurd."

She stared at him pointedly. "Joshua and Caleb after they saw the promised land?"

"Who are Joshua and Caleb?"

She shared a look with her father. "Never mind."

"No, tell me. Are Joshua and Caleb ranchers or farmers?

"They were Israelites Moses sent ahead to spy out the promised land after the people had been freed from bondage in Egypt," Irene supplied, surprising Elisabeth. "They returned saying the land God gave them flowed with milk and honey and that the bunches of grapes were so huge, it took two men to carry them."

Gabe nodded. "I've heard of Moses."

"The lesson to be learned," Sam said, "is that the other ten spies reported they'd seen giants. They thought it looked too risky to take over the land. They allowed fear to cloud their judgment, and their fear spread to the people. They wanted to tuck tail and run. What those ten spies had was an eye problem."

"What do you mean, Papa?" Phillip asked.

"They were looking at the circumstances with their

natural eyes and not eyes of faith. They said, 'We seemed like grasshoppers in our own eyes, and we looked the same to them.' But they were spies, sent to observe in secret. The giants didn't see them at all. Those men imagined their fears.''

"Tell about Joshua and Caleb," Anna said, leaning forward over her plate.

"Joshua and Caleb had a different perspective," Sam said. "God had, after all, promised that land to them. They gave Moses a good report about the lushness of the land."

"Maybe they hadn't seen the giants," Gabe suggested.

"Oh, they saw them all right. But they figured that if God had promised Canaan would be their home that those giants would either leave or be destroyed. They saw the same circumstances, but they saw them through God's promise and power. They said, 'Let's hurry on in there and take that land. We're well able to overcome and possess.'''

"What happened?" Gabe asked.

"All the people listened to the naysayers. They cried and complained and grumbled about Moses bringing them there and wished they had died in Egypt where they were slaves, and Joshua and Caleb couldn't talk them out of their fears. Even after God had parted the Red Sea for them and swallowed up the Egyptian army behind. Even though He dropped manna from the sky to feed them, still they didn't trust Him.

"So God said then that none of those over twenty years old would see the promised land. The ten spies

died from a plague. The people wandered in the wilderness for forty years until the last person, besides Joshua and Caleb, who'd been over twenty had died. Joshua and Caleb were allowed to enter Canaan.

"After that Joshua fought a lot of battles, and he's the one who led his army to march around Jericho until the walls fell."

"Tell us that story, Papa," Phillip encouraged.

"Another time," his father replied in a kind voice. "We've all had a long day and can all use some rest."

"Do you really believe in giants?" Gabe said later to Elisabeth as she reached to serve him rice pudding.

"There are several accounts in the Bible," she said. "Goliath was most likely a descendant of those giants the Israelites saw."

After Kalli, Elisabeth and Abigail had cleared away supper and finished the dishes, they joined the others in the great room where Anna sat working on her arithmetic and Sam held a twin on each knee. "Let's go up now so you can see your mother and Rachel for a few minutes," he said to the boys. "Then it's time for bed."

The younger siblings obediently joined him, and Kalli followed to help them prepare for bed, leaving Elisabeth with the Taggarts.

"Would you care for a game of cribbage?" she asked. "Or you're welcome to any of the books in Father's library down the hall."

"I believe I will get a book," Irene replied and left the room.

"Your father tells those stories as if they're real," Gabe said.

Elisabeth cast him a look. "They are real."

He said nothing.

Irene returned, book in hand. "You father has a copy of *The Memoirs of Uncle Tom*. I've never read it, but I've always wanted to."

"Sounds familiar," Gabe commented.

"It's Josiah Henson's personal telling of his life story. This is the book on which Harriet Beecher Stowe based *Uncle Tom's Cabin,* the book that practically started the war between the states by exposing the truth about slavery."

"I've always admired her," Elisabeth said. "She was a Christian lady. She met with Abraham Lincoln, you know."

"The female abolitionists are my role models," Irene told her with a nod. "By taking a stand for equality, they laid the groundwork for women's rights. I've heard Elizabeth Stanton and Matilda Joslyn Gage give speeches."

Gage looked at her with a brow cocked. "Where?"

"Our headmaster took all of us to Philadelphia for women's suffrage meetings whenever a speaker came through. This is an important year. While we're celebrating a hundred years of freedom, women still have fewer rights than their male counterparts. Did you realize that women do two-thirds of the work in our nation, but aren't even allowed the same legal privileges as men?"

"Which privileges are those?" he asked.

"Most importantly, the right to vote," she answered, sitting beside him. "This month the leaders of the suffrage movement are traveling in the states and territories, talking to the people. Women will be wearing black crepe on Independence Day to show their allegiance to the cause. In many cities and towns the women will the orators of the day." She turned to Elisabeth. "Why, I've attended so many meetings, *I* could give a speech!"

Gabe wanted to groan, but still absorbing this new information and a side of his sister he hadn't anticipated, he thought a moment before speaking. "It's all right for you to read your books and talk to us about this, but it might be better for everyone if you don't make your interest public."

Irene stared at him, disappointment in her expression, her stiff posture revealing anger.

Elisabeth cringed inwardly, waiting for her next words.

"Gabriel," Irene said in a controlled voice. "Are you going to tell me I can't stand up for what I believe?"

"No," he replied carefully. "I was just thinking how the single men would react to your passion for this cause. It might put them off."

"And why would I give a whit about what they think?"

"Because they're husband prospects."

This time she left the book on the sofa and stood. She took a step back as though he'd stung her. "It's your belief that I need a husband, therefore I should be compliant and pretend I'm someone I'm not in order to catch one?"

Elisabeth closed her eyes, feeling Irene's hurt. She

wished she could leave the room, but could hardly get up and run now.

"I didn't say that."

"You did say that." His sister pursed her lips, and then with more composure added, "You want to marry me off so I'm not a bother."

"No, Irene. It's not like that at all."

"Because I can support myself, you know. You paid for an education most young women never get. I can keep accounts, and I am familiar with many tasks. I could apprentice at a trade or I could be a bookkeeper. I even know enough about herbs and tinctures to help a doctor."

"That wasn't at all what I meant."

"What do you think, Elisabeth?" Irene asked, turning toward her. "Do you think women are entitled to have opinions about their own futures?"

Elisabeth didn't want to get in the middle of the siblings' disagreement. Neither did she want to take a side, but she sympathized with Irene and the hurt she was obviously feeling. "I understand that your brother has concerns for your future, and he feels a responsibility toward you. It's plain that he loves you."

Gabe seemed satisfied with her answer...but she continued.

"I don't necessarily agree with hiding your beliefs under a bushel just to please a prospective husband. You couldn't live your whole life stifled in that manner. When your true viewpoint became apparent, the man might feel as though he'd been tricked."

"As he would have been." Irene turned to Gabe again.

"And that is the life you'd have for me? Tricking a husband into marriage because who I really am isn't pleasing enough?"

He rubbed a palm down his face and cupped his jaw for a moment before dropping his hand. "The two of you have twisted my words into something I didn't intend."

"I can make my own decisions about my future," Irene said. "Without a man telling me what to do. You or any other man."

She turned on her heel and left the room.

Chapter Ten

Irene obviously hadn't wanted her brother to see her cry. Once she was gone, Elisabeth cast Gabe a tentative glance.

He looked as though he'd been shot again. "That wasn't what I intended."

"Her feelings are hurt," she told him. "She's only just arrived and you've told her you're planning to marry her off."

He shook his head. "No, I didn't say that."

"Not in those exact words, but you said it. It's plain she adores you. She's never had a family or a home. You're all she has, and if your main concern is for her to marry, she probably feels as though you don't want her with you."

"I do want her. I always wanted her. I was never able to take care of her, but I gave her the best education possible."

"Obviously. And now you don't want her to use it."

He sat forward with his elbows on his knees, head lowered, and laced his fingers in front of his eyes.

Elisabeth felt his pain as acutely as she'd felt Irene's. She moved to sit beside him and placed her hand on his shoulder.

He started at the touch, but turned his head to look at her. The anguish in his eyes told of his deep love and lack of confidence. He was so brash and smug in all other ways, this unfamiliar glimpse of vulnerability tugged at her heart.

"She loves you very much, Gabe. You're her only family in the world. Maybe she just wants to feel important in your eyes and have value. I've always had Father and my sisters, so I can't imagine what it would be like to spend Christmas and holidays without them and the knowledge that I belong. She needs to belong. You can give her that. You just have to be open."

He nodded, but didn't speak.

"I understand that you only want the best for her. You want to see her happy and fulfilled, and in your eyes marriage would be that fulfillment for her. Isn't that so?"

He nodded again.

"Just say it to her like that. Tell her you only want her to be happy. And that you'll support her in any manner that will bring her joy."

He lowered his hands and straightened. Elisabeth's hand, still on his shoulder, trailed down his back in a manner meant to be comforting.

Instead, he reached to take her by her upper arm and guide her closer to him. Her breath caught in her throat.

She'd never seen him in this light—and she liked the

evocative glimpse into his heart. There was something endearing about the man who clearly loved his sister, yet fumbled with how to communicate with her. He'd believed he'd done the best he could for Irene by placing her in a girls' academy, but what effect had the separation had on *him?* "Do you still believe you did the right thing for her by placing her in that school?"

"Sometimes I feel like I abandoned her, but it was because I wanted the best for her."

"Maybe she felt as though you abandoned her, too. Just ask."

"You make it sound easy."

"Nothing worthwhile is easy."

"Some things are," he replied.

Her gaze dropped to his mouth. Even though she knew the answer, she couldn't resist asking, "Like what?"

"Like kissing you." He leaned forward and covered her lips with his.

Elisabeth experienced a kind of giddy happiness she now associated with *this*—and with this man and the untried feelings his nearness and attention created. Gabe cupped her jaw, laced his fingers into her hair behind her ear and stroked his thumb over her cheekbone with aching gentleness.

The touch was so unlike anything she'd ever known or imagined, her breath caught in her throat. A realization flitted around her, daring her to take notice. There was something developing between them, something more than their initial butting of heads and his bold teasing. Her feelings about him had grown confusing, and she didn't like being uncertain about anything.

She had unconsciously moved her hand to his shoulder, and only now realized she was clinging to him a little too intensely. Embarrassed by her behavior, she drew back and sat away.

He studied her, but she let her gaze drop.

"Thanks," he said.

"For what?"

"For talking straight and pointing out what I'm too dense to figure out."

"That wasn't so hard, was it?" Again she turned his words back to him, and this time he grinned.

The fact that he'd been open to her suggestions touched her. Listening to advice seemed contrary to everything she'd learned about him until now, and the book of Proverbs came to mind. She remembered several verses about a man who sought counsel being wise. "You're not dense."

"Say it with more conviction."

She grinned. "You are not dense."

"I'll go talk to her. Which room?"

What he knew about talking to females he could've written on the palm of his hand. It didn't amount to much. He could stare a cold-blooded killer in the eye and not flinch. He was comfortable lying in wait for hours—sometimes days, without food and very little water—but he'd rather face off with a mama grizzly than see disillusionment or pain on his young sister's face. He was completely out of his element.

Elisabeth had made it all sound so simple. And maybe it was. But it sure wasn't comfortable.

He tapped on the door Elisabeth had pointed out.

"Who is it?" came the soft reply.

He would have opened the door to avoid the disruption in the hall since Mrs. Hart needed her rest, but his sister wasn't a child any longer. He couldn't just go barging in. "It's me," he said, holding his voice down.

A moment later, the door opened. He was thankful she didn't intend to ignore him. She had changed into her nightdress and a pale blue wrapper. Her feet were bare on the patterned rug. He followed her into the room and glanced around.

He recognized the straw hat perched on a metal sculptured stand atop a wardrobe. The unique scent of fresh linen and meadow grass unmistakably defined the room as Elisabeth's. Until that moment he hadn't realized how profoundly the woman disturbed him, but here he was recognizing her scent, identifying her belongings and experiencing an uneasy pull on his senses.

He focused on his sister. "We didn't get off to a very good start."

She sat on a chair and pointed to another beside a table in a slant-ceilinged dormer before several windows. "It wasn't the best news I've had, hearing you can't wait to get me out from underfoot when I've only just arrived."

How had he botched things so badly? "You're not underfoot and you never could be. I want you with me. The whole reason I came here and the reason I want to build a house is for you. For us. So we can be a family."

The tears that formed in her eyes made his chest ache. "Then why all this talk of being amenable to please and catch a husband?"

"I just thought—you're of an age when young ladies look for husbands, so I figured..." He stopped and shook his head. "I just want you to be happy. No matter what that means."

"I'm going to have plenty of time for all that to happen," she said. "And I don't want a husband who doesn't love me for who I am. I'm vocal about women's rights."

"I know that now."

"I wouldn't marry a man who opposed my convictions. If I marry, the man will have the same values and beliefs I do."

He didn't hold out for a man like that to turn up in Jackson Springs. He didn't need to voice his doubts, however. He was prepared to share a home with her forever. "Irene," he said.

She studied him.

"I never would have placed you in that school if I hadn't thought it was the best—and safest—place for you. I couldn't have paid for your education and the things you needed if I hadn't been able to travel."

"I believe you." She picked at a thread on the sleeve of her wrapper. "But I often wished you'd taken me with you. I'd have lived anywhere just to have been together."

The path he'd chosen had made that impossible. He'd spent over ten years chasing outlaws and staying alive by his wits and his skill with a gun. What he'd earned had been more than enough to fund boarding school; he'd lain by savings that would give them both a chance to start over. "What I did all those years was for us," he said. "For a future."

"Whenever you visited and I asked to come with you, you always said it wasn't possible. But you never told me what you did," she said. "And I guess I don't want to know if it was illegal."

She didn't know him. If he'd been in her place he'd have had plenty of doubts and suspicions…as well as questions. He didn't take her trust lightly. "It wasn't."

She folded her hands. "Good."

"Do you remember our parents?"

"Barely," she said. "I remember a big rocking chair by the fire, and Mother rocking me when I was small. I can picture our father in his white shirt and tie, and I recall him buying me licorice from a row of jars in a mercantile. What did he do?"

"He worked at the courthouse," Gabe replied.

"And they were killed by a horse and wagon?"

He nodded. "I was in school when the sheriff came for me. He took me to the undertaker's. That's where I last saw them. Mother had left you with a friend while the two of 'em went to lunch. Our house was in town and I suppose they did that on occasion. A team got startled in front of the livery and ran wild down the street. Smashed the wagon right up on the boardwalk and into the front of the building where they were sitting near the window."

"I vaguely remember staying with one family after another after that," she said.

He nodded. "Until I quit school and took a job at the livery so we could be together. Had a little room over the seamstress's shop."

"That must've been hard for you."

"Harder for you, probably. You were alone a lot. I couldn't take care of you by myself, feed you proper."

"I'm sorry," she said.

"For what?"

"That you had to quit school to take care of me."

"I was old enough," he told her. "No hardship. I just wanted you to have more than I could give you. So I saved enough to board you with a family, joined a drive and sent back everything I earned that first time. A couple years later I had enough to send you to the academy."

"Thank you, Gabriel."

"You don't owe me any thanks."

"I do. You took care of me."

"You're not obligated. It was my duty."

"You were just a boy yourself."

He shrugged. "We're here now."

"Can we start over?" she asked. "Fresh?"

Relieved, he nodded. "I'd like that."

She got up and knelt at his feet, where she laid her head on his knee. The warmth of her tears wet the fabric covering his leg. Hesitantly, he touched her hair and bent to place a kiss against her head. She looked up at him then, and her lashes glistened. "Thank you for bringing me here."

It took a minute for him to speak around the lump in

his throat. "It's what I always wanted. I was just waiting for the time to be right."

She smiled.

"The house will be serviceable and you'll be comfortable," he told her. "But don't expect it to be like this one." He glanced around the room.

"This place is something else, isn't it? And the Harts are such generous people. Elisabeth is sleeping with her sister tonight so I can have this room."

"They're good people," he replied.

"So she nursed you for the past week?" she asked.

He nodded. "Somewhat begrudgingly, to be sure."

"I can hardly believe that."

"We didn't get off to a good start."

"And now?"

He thought over their relationship. "She's tolerating me."

"I think she more than tolerates you."

"What do you mean?"

"When she thinks no one is looking—when you're not looking—she casts telling glances your way. And *you…*" Wearing a teasing smile, she gathered her robe around her legs and pushed to her feet. "The looks you give her say more than 'please pass the mashed potatoes.'"

He had no reply. He didn't know what he thought about Elisabeth, and he didn't want to examine his feelings. The notion that anyone else had glimpsed his confusing attraction to her didn't sit well. He stood. "I'd better go so you can get some rest."

"Good night, Gabriel." She stepped against him and

laid her head against his chest. "Everything's going to be grand now that we're together."

He returned her hug. One of his concerns had been set to rest. Irene didn't intend to pressure him to tell her how or where he'd made his living up until now. And if she did learn somehow, he was relatively certain she wouldn't be appalled or fault-finding. Still, he didn't want to risk losing her esteem.

Three gas lamps lit the long hallway, and in their glow, he spotted Elisabeth perched on a bench beneath a window. Behind her the night sky was dark and the moon filtered through the swaying branches of a tree. She'd freed her hair from its braid and the shiny mass hung down her back in ripples.

He strode toward her and she got to her feet.

"I don't mean to be intrusive, but I can't help wondering how it went," she whispered.

"Don't want to wake your family," he replied.

She glanced aside and then gestured. "Up here."

He followed her to what appeared as another room, but instead the door led up a narrow set of stairs to another door, which she opened and entered through. She lit a lamp, illuminating a tiny square room furnished with undersize chairs, enormous pillows and bookcases filled with books and dolls.

She closed the door. "This has always been a hideaway for we three sisters," she said. "The boys aren't allowed. I still come here when the household is chaotic and I want to be alone." She took a seat on one of the chairs and gestured for him to join her. "The few times my father's been in here, he used the cushions."

He had his doubts about the spindly little chairs holding his weight, so Gabe seated himself and hoped he could get back up without embarrassing himself. "I said the same things to Irene that I said to you."

"And she forgave you and you made up."

"More or less." He looked toward a window. "Thanks to you and your insight."

"It wasn't all that difficult to recognize her feelings. Or yours."

He faced her. "What am I feeling now?"

Chapter Eleven

She shrugged and a long skein of hair fell forward over her shoulder. "Relief? Regret maybe."

"Thank you for giving up your room so Irene could sleep in there."

"I don't mind sleeping with Anna. She thinks it's great fun when we have a lot of company and share rooms." She sat with her hands in the pockets of her robe and a clicking sound came from the one on the right.

Curious, Gabe glanced at her lap.

She withdrew her hand to show him what she held: three small smooth stones. He frowned in puzzlement.

"I have a collection of stones," she explained. "I gathered them along riverbanks and on the prairies as we traveled west with our wagon train. At first I just liked them and thought it would be fun to save mementos from along the trail." She held her hand open and studied the three rocks. "They've become reminders of the sacrifice we made to come here...of losing my mother.

They remind me that the decisions we make have ever-lasting repercussions."

He understood that. He'd chosen to hunt down wanted men. He was good at it, and the bounties had been more than he could have made any other way. At the time it had seemed like the best choice…but now he had to live with the lives that had been changed—and lost—along the way. Now he had to keep his past a secret from civilized people like these.

"You get those out and look at them often?"

"I have a few with me all the time," she replied with a sheepish glance through her lashes. "These have been in the pocket of my wrapper."

"Imagine they're a good reminder to think before you do somethin' you'll regret." Though he doubted she needed the rocks. She seemed pretty set on doing what was right as a way of life.

She stared at the trio of stones in her palm for a long minute, and at last took a deep breath. She extended her hand. "Pick one."

He gave her a curious glance. Was this some sort of game?

"Go ahead," she coaxed. "Take one."

He plucked one with an interesting smooth divot from her hand. "Now what?"

"Now put it in your pocket. It's yours."

The gesture caught him off guard. The rocks obviously held great sentiment. "Thank you. Irene's the only one who's ever given me a gift."

She tilted her head to ask, "Are you poking fun at me? It wasn't a gold watch."

"Not at all." His voice was low. As a child his sister had drawn him pictures and once, in subsequent years, had sewn him a shirt that was too small. He still had it, though.

He closed his hand over the warm stone.

She pushed to her feet. "I have a notary job in the judge's chambers at the courthouse early tomorrow, so I'd better get some sleep."

"I'll be ordering lumber and getting supplies," he said. "Will Irene be all right staying here?"

"She can come with me," Elisabeth said. "She'll enjoy my meeting. The Tanners are adopting a little boy. This is only the second adoption I've witnessed, but it's a joyful event watching a family form. Last time I cried."

He grinned. "I'm sure she'll be glad to go with you. Do you have a key to the house we're moving into? I can have our things moved."

"It's in the carved teakwood box on the foyer table."

He had to stop at the bank to check on how his money transfer had progressed. He wanted to pay the Harts for food and lodging. Which gave him an idea for something to occupy Irene.

He held his side while he rose from the cushions.

They both reached for the doorknob at the same time, and her hand covered the back of his. She surprised him by not pulling hers away.

They stood like that, with his heart beating so hard he wondered if she could hear it and her shoulder touching his chest. Beneath his chin, her hair was as fragrant as he remembered. Without planning to, he raised his other hand to thread his fingers through the length of her cool silken hair.

Without preamble, she turned and was in his arms, her face raised to his expectantly.

She smelled better than a meadow full of wildflowers on a spring day. Better than fresh linens and new mown hay. Her own unique scent clung to her and filled his senses.

He still held the stone. The stone that was supposed to remind him of the consequences of choices. What could come of holding this young woman in his arms? What lasting ramifications would result from kissing her…from allowing himself these moments of sweet affection?

They were as far apart in experience and points of view as a mountain peak and a gorge. She was pure and filled with hope and promise, and he was a cynic who'd seen the worst of people and looked for trouble behind every tree. She'd been raised in the lap of a kind and God-fearing family, while he'd lived a solitary existence on guts and sheer determination. She possessed a stalwart faith he couldn't comprehend. Gabe, on the other hand, figured if there was a God up there, he'd done nothing to deserve any special consideration.

The stone was practically burning his hand.

Her eyes were as blue as the wildflowers down Texas way.

He dropped the rock into his pocket and placed that hand on her shoulder, trapping silken hair in his gentle hold.

The way she looked at him showed she was as uncertain about whatever it was that had been developing between them as he was, but she showed no fear or hesitation. If she had, he couldn't have taken her in his embrace and kissed her the way he did, with the joy of discovery and never-before-known wonder beating in his heart.

Had she shown any reluctance or resisted he'd have backed away and forgotten the idea, but she didn't. She seemed every bit as curious as he to examine the new and mystifying feelings.

He probably liked kissing her too much. He was certain he wasn't on her list of eligible men, and she…well he had too many other problems to take care of without adding this one to the list.

Didn't he?

The following morning, Irene had telegrams to send. "I'm contacting the governor of the Colorado Territory as well as the administrator of the Christian Women's Liberty Union. There's no reason why one of the spokespersons can't be here on Independence Day. It will add another dimension to the celebration."

"You know who to contact to make an arrangement like that?" Elisabeth asked.

"When in doubt, go to the top," she replied.

After Elisabeth checked her timepiece brooch, they headed for the courthouse.

"I admire your job," Irene told her. "Are there other women notaries?"

"I'm sure there are," Elisabeth replied. "If not many,

the most likely deterrent is the travel. I take the train, and up until this last time it has been safe."

"How did it happen?" Irene asked. "I never heard all the details about the train robbery, and I want to know."

Elisabeth shared her account, not sparing the uncomfortable truth regarding her reluctance to part with her mother's ring and how it escalated the situation.

"I understand your attachment," Irene told her. "I have only a few things that belonged to my mother, and I would never part with them. Not even at gunpoint." They paused on a corner. "How did your mother die?"

She rarely spoke of that day. On occasion when one of Elisabeth's sisters brought it up, they talked about their fear and grief. But Elisabeth harbored more than grief. It was her fault their father hadn't gone in search of his wife when they'd been cast into the river. Elisabeth had been so terrified, that even though she'd been able to reach an overhanging branch and cling to it for dear life, she'd screamed in terror for help until her father had come for her.

If he'd gone for her mother first, they'd both have been saved.

She shared the story without those disturbing details, however.

"I wasn't as old as you when my mother died," Irene said. "But still I've missed her my whole life. I wasn't right there when it happened, either. I can't imagine how difficult her death has been for you."

"Thank you," Elisabeth said. By then they'd reached

their destination, and she'd talked about the subject more than enough.

Half an hour later, Elisabeth and Irene left the courthouse with buoyant spirits. "Shall we stop at the café for tea and biscuits?" Elisabeth asked. "It's not exactly like the teahouses in Denver, but regardless, the tea is good."

"I would like that."

Penelope Berry greeted them. Irene balked at taking the table in front of the window, so they took seats in the back of the room. Elisabeth had never had close friends her own age. Her younger sisters had always kept her company, and she'd never questioned her friendless situation because she was content. Her classmates had been silly creatures, chattering about the boys and their dresses and hair, while Elisabeth had turned her focus squarely on her studies.

She'd never taken an interest in what she considered the foolish ways of other females. That's why her enjoyment of Irene's company puzzled her. But as far as she'd seen, Irene wasn't silly or obsessed with her hair or clothing. She had an enviable education, a fluent vocabulary and a knowledge of history and society that Elisabeth admired.

She had liked Irene from the first, and the more she got to know her, the more impressed she was. She'd never seen the need for a friend, never sought a companion or prayed for friends, but God seemed to have anticipated her needs and sent Irene anyway.

She still didn't hold as much appreciation for Gabe's presence in Jackson Springs as she did his sister's, but she now suspected that his arrival and the land he owned had been determined by God's hand and wisdom.

"I have prayed for Gabriel for many years," Irene mentioned now. "For his safety, of course, but also that God would lead him to a time and a place where we could be a family. Now God has answered my prayers and brought us here."

Elisabeth had discovered that many people never mentioned God in their everyday conversations, but those who had a personal relationship with Him spoke of Him as naturally as they spoke of their friends and family. At the confirmation of Irene's faith, her fondness for the other woman grew yet again. *Thank You, Lord. Thank You for a friend.*

She hadn't realized how much time had passed or that other customers were now filling the café and ordering lunch. "I would suggest we stay to eat, but I want to get home and see to my stepmother."

They paid and headed for the door. Just as they stepped out onto the boardwalk, Rhys Jackson greeted them. "Good day, Elisabeth." He glanced at Irene and removed his bowler. "Afternoon, miss."

"Rhys, this is Irene Taggart. Irene, this is a good friend of our family, Rhys Jackson."

"How do you do?" he said with avid appreciation shining in his eyes. "It's a pleasure to make your acquaintance." His expression barely faltered. Irene wouldn't have noticed the new interest Elisabeth recognized. "Taggart, you say?"

"Have you met my brother?"

His eyes lit up. "Indeed I have. And to what does Jackson Springs owe the pleasure of your visit?"

"Oh, I'm not visiting, Mr. Jackson. I'm now a resident. As we speak, Gabriel is seeing to building us a home nearby."

"In town?"

"About three quarters of a mile to the northwest," Elisabeth supplied. "A handsome parcel of land with meadows and a stream flowing from the mountains. Gabe has already selected the location for the house."

"Indeed. Well, welcome to Jackson Springs, Miss Taggart. Good day, Elisabeth."

As soon as he'd entered the café, Irene asked, "Jackson?"

Elisabeth nodded. "His grandfather founded our community and many of the businesses. Rhys and his mother own the bank."

"The people are certainly friendly. I think I'm going to like it here."

Stepping off the boardwalk, they headed for home.

Elisabeth found her stepmother sitting in a chair in her bedroom, the loosely wrapped infant in her arms.

"How are the two of you?" Elisabeth asked.

"We're doing well," Josie replied.

"What can I do for you?"

"I'd really love to take a bath and wash my hair," Josie replied hopefully. "I didn't want to ask Kalli to care for the baby. She has her hands full with the twins, and besides…I don't know that she has experience with one so small."

"Rachel and I would love to get acquainted while you bathe. Just let me go heat water and fill the tub. I'll be right back."

Nearly half an hour later, she returned for the baby who was now awake.

"She just nursed, so she should be all right until I return."

"Don't worry about us." Elisabeth took the tiny warm bundle into her arms and beheld her with affection. It never failed to astound her how perfectly a baby was created and how incredibly tiny and helpless they were. Rachel had straight dark hair that stood off the top of her head and fell forward onto her forehead. It was silky to the touch, and when Elisabeth ran a fingertip down her cheek, she was struck anew by the incredible softness of the baby's skin.

She'd been fourteen when Phillip had been born, seventeen when the twins arrived, yet even as a girl she'd felt this stirring awe and fathomless love for each of her younger siblings. Elisabeth touched her lips to the baby's forehead and inhaled her newborn scent.

In coloring, Rachel took after Elisabeth's father, like the twins. Seeing who a child would resemble particularly fascinated Elisabeth. Each child was a glorious and unique gift, created in a wondrous way. For the first time she wondered what it would be like to have her own child, to hold a baby she'd carried inside her... to recognize hair and features of a husband.

Unexpectedly a picture of Gabe flashed in her mind's eye.

Chapter Twelve

Gabe had hair as dark as her father's…he was tall…handsome. Any child he fathered would be as pretty as this one—what was she doing?

Elisabeth had to corral those thoughts and focus on something more appropriate—and logical. She took a seat in the rocker and hummed until Josie returned, dressed and with damp hair.

How are our guests faring?" she asked. "I was disappointed I missed Gabe's sister's arrival. Your father told me about dinner."

"It was lively," she answered. "I really like her. She's smart and she doesn't carry on about fashion and social functions like most of the young women I know. Gabe is having their things moved into the parsonage today, though. I was thinking that while Rachel sleeps, I'll go down and help Irene get settled."

"Rachel won't sleep but a couple of hours at a time just yet," Josie told her. "And when she's awake each time she'll only want me." She smiled. "So you go ahead and we'll do just fine. You don't have to wait on me. Your father walks up the hill and checks on us every few hours. He wanted to stay home, but I told him definitely not." She smiled. "He has a tendency to hover."

"He's a wonderful father," Elisabeth said.

Her stepmother agreed. "And a wonderful husband." Josie opened the window wider and stood in a shaft of sunlight so her hair would dry more quickly. "I still remember the first time I met all of you. My heart went out to you over your loss, and Sam was so sad and blamed himself for your mother's death. He loved her so much…his love was plain in everything he said and did—and in what he didn't say or do. I yearned for a love like that. For acceptance. I never thought I'd have it for myself. And I never dreamed he would be able to love again…to love me."

"He loves you very much," Elisabeth said. "It took me a while to understand love has no limits. We aren't created to love only a certain number of people and then our love's used up. Loving you didn't mean he didn't love my mother and it didn't take anything away from her. He wasn't loving you *instead* of her."

Josie turned to look at her, and tears escaped over her lower lids to her cheek. She brushed them away quickly.

"I didn't mean to make you cry."

Josie emitted a little laugh that sounded like a sob. "Everything is going to make me cry for a few weeks. It's okay."

She took Rachel from Elisabeth and placed her in her cradle.

"I am only just beginning to see something else," Elisabeth said.

"What's that?"

"I always thought your marriage was convenient. Father married you because he needed a wife and we needed a mother."

"I was so happy to have a family that I could have accepted that," she replied.

"But he *loves* you, doesn't he?" She studied her stepmother. "I mean it started out like that and love developed. Fondness, appreciation, all that. But it didn't stop there. I don't know what I'm trying to say."

"I do." Josie came to stand in front of her. "We fell *in* love."

Elisabeth nodded. "Yes."

"Couples have had arranged marriages since Bible times—not so much arranged as bargained for and given in trade. I have to wonder how many of those ended as well as ours. I fancied myself in love with my first husband before I married him, and I lived a lonely existence as his wife."

"Were you brokenhearted when he died?"

"I was brokenhearted while he was still alive," she answered.

"How can a person know if it's going to turn out badly?"

"You can't, sweetie. You just have to ask the good Lord to send you the right one and then trust Him."

"I know that if I do marry, I want a man just like Father."

Josie touched her cheek. "He is indeed a very good

example of a loving husband and kind father. That's a pretty tall order."

"Not too big for God," Elisabeth replied. "He did it for you."

Josie smiled. "Indeed He did." She gave Elisabeth a gentle hug. "You run along and help Irene now."

Elisabeth gave her a smile and enjoyed looking at Rachel one more time. "My new sister sure is pretty."

Josie got tears in her eyes again and shooed her off.

That afternoon, Elisabeth assisted Irene in arranging the furniture in the tiny little house to her liking, unpacking and storing away Irene's belongings and shopping for food. Once the items were all put away, Irene looked around the kitchen. "I guess I'd better think of what I'll prepare Gabriel for supper."

"I had planned for you to eat with us," Elisabeth said. "You can get more practice before doing it all yourself. I don't know how much help I'll be advising you on your cooking. I've never had less than five or six people to prepare for, and it's often more than that. Maybe Josie can give you advice."

Everything was finished then, except Gabe's saddle bags, a valise and a wooden crate, which stood untouched against a wall in the tiny room he would be using. The two women stood staring at them.

"Do you want to unpack his things?" Elisabeth asked finally.

Irene glanced at her and then back. She shook her head.

The thought of going through Gabe's personal belongings didn't sit well with Elisabeth, either, so Irene's head shake brought her relief.

An hour later, they were back up the hill.

For the next few days Gabe stayed busy locating carpenters and having the materials delivered to the site of the Taggarts' future home. Irene accompanied Elisabeth and assisted her in the church office, which made the chores go more quickly and gave Elisabeth more time at the house with Josie and the baby.

"I can't trail you everywhere you go forever," Irene said thoughtfully on Friday afternoon. "I graduated several weeks ago, of course, but before that I was used to attending classes and studying. Right now there's not all that much for me to do while Gabriel is working. The house is tiny and doesn't take much upkeep. I don't fancy standing in the kitchen baking."

"You could certainly continue a study that interests you," Elisabeth suggested. "You've been a big help to me with my father's research. History, perhaps, or a Bible course. I know many subjects interest you, but is there anything you'd like to pursue? Do you paint or write poetry?"

"I am interested in government," she answered. "For example I've spoken with a few people lately, regarding the fact that this territory hasn't achieved statehood. It's a subject close to many citizens' hearts. Perhaps I could learn the steps that have been taken and petition the president."

Her idea, as lofty as it seemed to Elisabeth, was indeed a good one. Unlike Irene's eagerness for women to have the right to vote, this cause would garner support.

"Are there any women on the town council…or on the board of governors of the territory?"

"I couldn't say for certain, but it's not likely," Elisabeth replied.

"I've contacted several of my acquaintances, and I'm relatively positive we'll have a well-known suffragette here to make a speech on Independence Day. I'm quite persuasive."

Elisabeth had never been one to make waves, so she admired Irene for her unflagging zeal and for not being afraid to state her beliefs or to take a stand for them. Elisabeth believed women deserved as many rights as their male counterparts, as well. She needed to follow Irene's example and not be too timid to do the right thing if the time ever arose.

"I admire you," she told her new friend. "And I think you're going to be a positive addition to Jackson Springs whatever you decide to do."

The Stellings had been invited for dinner well in advance of Rachel's arrival, and Josie insisted they continue with their plans. She trusted her stepdaughters and Irene to plan and prepare the meal, and she joined the others in the dining room, Rachel in her arms.

Sam had cleaned up the small crib that fit at the end of the room and became a fixture in their dining whenever they had a new baby. Elisabeth had washed fresh bedding and affixed a rag doll Anna had offered to the side. Josie smiled with delight when she saw the bed, and after Arlene and her daughters had admired Rachel's silky hair and tiny fingers, she gently laid her down.

Josie made appropriate introductions before taking

her seat beside her husband, introducing their dear friends to the Taggarts. "When the Harts had first arrived in Jackson Springs, the Stellings were some of our first friends," she explained. "Chess and Arlene helped us make the adjustment to our new home. Elisabeth and Gilbert studied together and have been friends. And Abigail and Anna took right to Libby and Patience and have been chums ever since."

"Gilbert is our deputy marshal," Sam mentioned for Irene's benefit. Gabe had already met him.

"You're kind to call it studying together, Mrs. Hart," Gil said with a grin. "Truth is Lis tutored me so I could pass my English classes. I still can't tell you when to use lay, lie or laid."

Gabe took a bowl of mashed potatoes Irene passed to him, but his focus had been snared by the information about the deputy and his friendship with Elisabeth. Gil sat directly across from Gabe, with Elisabeth at his side. He observed as they took portions of food and interacted.

"Did you make these creamed carrots?" Gil asked.

"Are they still your favorites?"

He grinned. "Yes."

"Then I made them."

They shared a quiet laugh.

Gabe finally noticed Libby waiting for the mashed potatoes and handed her the bowl. "Abby and Anna told us all about how you prevented those robbers from getting their mama's ring," she said to him. "Elisabeth sets great store by that ring, so I know how much she

appreciated you coming to her rescue like that. It was a very brave thing you did."

Uncomfortable with the subject, he decided explanations would only draw more attention. He was at a loss for a reply, and she was waiting. "Miss Hart does favor that ring."

"Do you have anything special that belonged to your mother?" she asked.

"Well…" He thought a few seconds. "I have a tintype of my parents on their wedding day. And some books…and a silver comb and brush set I've been saving for Irene. Guess she can have it now that she's not at school."

"You never mentioned that, Gabriel," Irene said from his other side. "Where are they? When can I see them?"

"They're in those crates in my room. Station delivered them a couple days ago. Had 'em stored all these years."

"You'll have to sort all that out yourself," she said. "Elisabeth and I didn't touch your things."

"I wouldn't have cared." He glanced at Elisabeth. "But I can take care of it."

Gil's parents, seated at Sam's right side and across from Josie, were engaged in a conversation with their hosts. Patience, Anna and Abigail held their own quiet conversation, which left Libby free to ask him more questions.

Gil glanced over a couple of times, and he and Elisabeth shared a look. It wasn't until that moment that Gabe realized Libby had been flirting with him all along, engaging him in conversation and showing avid interest.

"How old is Libby?" he whispered to his sister when no one else was paying attention.

"She's out of school, so maybe eighteen?" She gave him a curious look. "Why?"

He simply tilted his head to indicate he was merely curious and tasted the creamed carrots.

"Josie tells me you're building a house," Arlene Stelling said to Gabe.

He glanced from Gil to his mother beside him. "The work will get underway next week," he told her.

"Gil has mentioned getting a house of his own," she said. "Do you want one that's all ready to move into or will you build a new place?"

Gil shrugged. "I don't know. I don't need a very big place or anything special."

"You'll have a wife one of these days," his mother reminded him. "Maybe you do need something special."

"I guess I'll figure that out when it happens."

Elisabeth didn't blush or glance at him as though that idea held any significance for her. She asked Kalli to pass the bread, which had ended up on the far end of the table by the boys.

"Are there many homes available?" Irene asked.

"There must be enough to keep Thomas Payne in business," Sam replied. "He handles local real estate."

"Daisy Martin and her family moved to Denver," Abigail said. "They had a nice house on Spencer Street.

The brick one with the porch and the foliage that grows up the chimney."

"That house is empty?" Gil asked. "I remember going to birthday parties there when we were kids. Remember, Lis?"

Elisabeth nodded. "It has a great big kitchen. Mrs. Martin had it painted bright yellow."

Gil's expression showed interest. "Maybe I'll visit Tom and ask to see the place."

"My schedule is open," Irene said with a grin. "I'm available to go with you."

Several sets of eyes turned to Irene.

"If you'd like company, that is," she added. "I was just thinking…I'm free and all. I could give you a woman's perspective."

Gil's parents deliberately surveyed their plates. Elisabeth locked gazes with Josie for the briefest of moments. Gabe turned to look at Irene beside him. Her cheeks were flushed, and she wore a hesitant smile. Now *she* was flirting! Right in plain sight of everyone at the dinner table.

Gil returned her smile with a hesitation, but interest. "That would be nice," he said finally. "I'll talk to Tom and let you know." Then he glanced aside, as though he didn't want anyone to get the wrong idea. "Anyone else want to come along?"

No one took him up on the offer.

"Lis?" he asked, looking directly at her.

"It would depend on my schedule," she replied. "If I don't have an appointment, I can join you."

After they'd finished eating, Sam asked Abigail and

Anna to clean up the dishes. Elisabeth and Patience joined them. Josie directed the others into the great room.

"Remember when we were the ones doing the dishes?" Arlene took Rachel from Josie's arms. "Now we have all these grown children."

"Children are a blessing from the Lord," Josie agreed.

Gabe got his first good look at the baby as Arlene uncovered her scrawny legs and held her for Chess to see. "Can you remember when our babies were this tiny?"

"At that size I was scared to death of 'em," the man replied. "Still am."

"The girls keep a checkerboard in that side table drawer," Gil said to Irene. "How is your game?"

She gave him a warning look. "I have skills that will amaze you."

Obviously familiar with the room and comfortable helping himself as though he'd done it a hundred times, Gil found the board and disks and set up the game on the side table, then arranged chairs for the two of them on either side.

Libby took a chair across from where Gabe sat on a divan. "If their game doesn't last too long, perhaps you'd like to play."

Chapter Thirteen

"I don't know how."

Her eyebrows shot up. "You've never played checkers?"

"Nope."

"I can teach you."

If this was what civilized people did after dinner, he guessed he might as well learn. "Okay." And realizing polite conversation was expected, he came up with a question. "Do you...are you involved in any studies?"

"Studies. Like school? No, I graduated two years ago. I now work for Opal Zimmerman, the dressmaker."

"Oh. Do a lot of women need dresses?"

"All women need dresses. Some more than others. Coats, too. I only just made my first coat. It's in the window at the shop if you should walk past."

"I'll have a look."

"Appears you're healing," Chess said then, taking the seat beside him. "Feeling better, are you?"

"Much better," Gabe replied, relieved to have another

person join the conversation. "I've been riding, and it's getting easier."

"I broke ribs once, and you couldn't have made me get on a horse," Chess told him.

"He didn't have any trouble coming to the dinner table, though," his wife remarked, eliciting a laugh from those nearby.

"Well, this one's cracked, so it's probably not as painful," Gabe said in the man's defense.

Chess gestured to Gabe and tilted his head at his wife. "You see?" He grinned. "At any rate it's good to see you doing well. Last Sunday you were still lying abed, but I reckon we'll see you at church day after next."

"Church?" Gabe glanced from the man to his hosts, who were smiling encouragement. He'd been taken in by the minister's family. Of course they'd expect him to come to church. "Well, I—"

"We're looking forward to services," Irene said. "If we ever attended church together before, I was too young to remember. I can't wait to meet more residents of Jackson Springs, especially if they're all as nice as those I've met so far." She gave Gil another meaningful glance.

Elisabeth entered the room in time to pick up on the topic. "Father is an inspiring preacher. He plans his sermons for days, sometimes weeks in advance, and delivers them with conviction and compassion."

Sam caught her hand. "Elisabeth is my right hand. She sees to all the tasks that would keep my attention from preparing lessons or seeing to the spiritual needs of the congregation."

"Don't glorify straightening hymnals and baking communion bread."

Sam looked straight at Gabe. "She's humble. She does a great deal of research for me, finding scriptures I need and locating details of history and Bible interpretation in my library. She used to do all the cleaning and preparing of communion, too, but now she delegates those jobs. She even counts the tithes and offerings and makes the bank deposit each week. And she often accompanies me to visit the sick and elderly."

Gabe had never even thought about all the work that went into being a preacher. He'd seen how much Elisabeth did in this home, what with sharing meal preparations and changing bedding. In addition she managed to fit in her notary duties.

She was of an age to marry. Considering all her attributes, it was a wonder no man had offered for her yet. Perhaps the idea of marriage didn't appeal to her.

He studied Irene and Gil at their checker game. Why hadn't Gil proposed to her? Why hadn't the banker? Maybe one of them had and she'd turned him down. Elisabeth seemed as headstrong as his sister.

"Each one of my children is a blessing," Sam assured them. "Each unique and special in his or her own way."

"And now you have yet another blessing," Arlene Stelling said with a warm smile.

"My cup runneth over." Sam looked directly at his wife as he said the last.

More than once Gabe had picked up on the looks that passed between them. They shared something special. Something unfamiliar in his experience. As unfamiliar as attending church. He didn't want to let on to Irene that he hadn't set foot inside a church since their parents' funerals. She took God as seriously as these others did, and he didn't want to appear the only heathen in their midst.

An hour later, Elisabeth got up. "I'll set dessert and coffee out on the sideboard in the dining room. Once I have it ready, you can eat in there or bring your plates and cups in here." She turned directly to John and Peter, who had arranged their blocks into corrals for their toy horses. "That doesn't include you boys. You will eat at your usual places."

She glanced around and Gabe figured she was looking for help. A couple of the girls had only returned from finishing supper dishes and cleanup a few minutes ago, and Irene was still occupied at the checkerboard.

"I'll help," Gabe said.

His offer caught her by surprise. "You?"

"I have two hands."

"Of course. All right then, thank you."

In the kitchen, she heated the coffee she'd made earlier and pointed to a cupboard. "The dessert plates are in there."

He opened it and figured the smaller ones were dessert plates. "How many?"

"All of them."

He lifted them out. "Dining room?"

"On the sideboard please."

He delivered them and returned. "Are you disturbed about Irene making friends with your deputy?"

"Not at all, and he's not *my* deputy."

"But there's something between the two of you, isn't there?"

She uncovered two baking dishes that held something with a golden crust. "Something like what?" She glanced up. Her expression changed to one of surprise. "Do you mean...romantic? Goodness, no. Gilbert and I are friends, and that's the extent of it. I have never considered him in any other way."

"What about him? Maybe he has designs on you, but he doesn't let on."

She shook her head. "No," she said firmly. "It's not like that. We've always had an easy, comfortable association. Anything else would ruin that. Huh-uh. If you had any inkling that he took a romantic interest in me, how would you account for the rapt attention he's been paying your sister all evening?"

"You noticed?"

"It would be difficult not to notice. They've been making eyes at each other and *smiling*." She gave an impression of a silly smile.

"I was afraid of that."

"Of what?"

"He isn't the sort I'd want to see her involved with."

She stopped in the middle of reaching for a china sugar bowl. "Why ever not?" she asked as though he'd personally insulted her. "Gilbert's a trustworthy and honest person. He's a deputy, for goodness' sake. What does that say about his character? He's kind to his sisters and good to his parents and he's a very loyal friend. He attends church every Sunday, unless he's on duty at the jail, and he's not hard to look at. He's rather handsome actually."

"I'm sure he is all of those things you say," he told her. "It's the deputy part that bothers me. If she was to marry him—and I'm not saying that after one evening and a checker game she's going to marry him—but if she did…a lawman's job is dangerous. I wouldn't choose a lawman for her."

She poured fresh cream into a small pitcher that matched the sugar bowl. "Well, it's not up to you, now is it?"

He should have guessed she wouldn't see the subject from his perspective. He'd be hard-pressed to think of anything they'd agreed upon yet. "That Jackson fellow," he said. "Now he has a safe job at the bank. Unless of course…*he's* the one you have your sights set on."

"Again," she said, "if you start pressing her toward marriage or a husband she doesn't select for herself, you will push her away." She placed a handful of forks on the tray beside the cream and sugar. "And just how many more men can you imagine pairing me with?"

"He does have designs on you," Gabe said. "I saw it."

"I've never encouraged him." She hadn't denied Jackson's attraction to her, only her encouragement. "You flatter me if you think every man in town finds me irresistible."

Odd, the relief he'd experienced at her denial on both counts. "I can only think you have discouraged them because of your desire for independence, because you'd make any one of them a good wife."

She had picked up the tray, but she paused with it hovering inches over the table. "If God shows me a man He wants me to marry, I'll consider it then."

"How will you know?"

She looked down. "Can we finish this conversation later? I need to set out dessert before the boys have to go to bed."

"We don't have to talk about it at all if you don't want to."

She met his eyes briefly and headed for the dining room.

He appreciated her advice regarding his sister. She understood females far better than he did. The last thing he wanted was to offend Irene again, but if she took a shine to the deputy, he was going to have a rough time keeping his nose out of it. For now, he would stay in the background and see what happened. Except...

"If she goes to see the house with the deputy, go along, will you, please?"

Her eyes held humor when she looked at him. "It was the *please* that got me. Yes, I will accompany her."

"Thanks." He held up a hand before she could say it. "No, that wasn't hard at all. Thank you. See?"

Her laugh melted something inside him.

Later that night after they'd arrived at the tiny house and Irene had gone to her room, he pried lids from the crates. Minutes later she opened her door to his knock.

"I found these for you."

Her gaze dropped to the silver-handled comb, brush and mirror he held. Tears welled in her eyes. "Oh, Gabriel."

"They're tarnished."

"I'll polish them." She accepted the set, carried them into her room and placed them on the bureau before turning back.

"Thank you for saving them for me all this time." She wrapped her arms around his neck and hugged him soundly. "I prayed for this time to come. I prayed that God would keep you safe all those years, and He did. Even if we never got a bigger house, even if we lived here forever, I'd be content."

If there was a God, Gabe figured he was on the bottom of the list as far as prayers went, so his safety had to have been purely by coincidence and sheer wit. "We're getting a bigger house."

Before the service began Sunday morning, Elisabeth was tying Peter's shoe for the third time when the hum of conversation faded out, and the sanctuary grew unusually quiet. She glanced up, noting heads turning toward the rear of the building. Conversation buzzed again, this time with excitement.

"That's him, the man who saved the whole car full of people from the robbers."

"The Taggart fellow is more handsome than I expected."

"Is that his wife?"

"No, I heard his sister has joined him."

Elisabeth got to her feet and helped Peter get situated

with the rest of family in the two front rows. She turned then, spotting Gabe and Irene as half a dozen people greeted them just inside the doors. Though it was a warm morning, Gabe wore a dark jacket over his white shirt and string tie. He held his hat in both hands, worrying the brim in a circle, his discomfort evident. She hurried to extricate the two of them from the gathering, showed him where to hang his hat, and ushered them to the join the rest of the Harts.

Just as they took their seats, the strains of the first hymn came from the organ as Constance Graham opened the service with *A Mighty Fortress Is Our God* and the choir led the singing. Voices rose around them, the various sopranos and baritones blending into a joyful chorus of praise. Elisabeth's father stood at the podium, his smile showing his pleasure at the sizeable turnout that morning.

About halfway through the last song, the doors at the rear of the sanctuary burst open.

Music and song came to an abrupt halt.

"There's trouble over at Doc Barnes's place!" the out-of-breath man in the doorway shouted. "A bunch o' rowdy good-for-nuthins are holding him at gunpoint! The marshal needs a few guns."

Heart pounding, Elisabeth scanned the room. The Stellings sat on the opposite side, a few rows back. Gil wasn't with them. "Oh, dear Lord," she whispered.

Gil's cousin, Will York, shot out of his seat and immediately ran for the door. Dan Larken, another deputy, made his way past his concerned-looking wife and son seated on the pew, and his father, Victor, joined him.

Warren Burke, the livery owner, stood, too. Rhys remained seated beside Beatrice.

Behind Elisabeth, Irene said, "No," and Elisabeth turned as Gabe rose to his full stature and stepped into the aisle. "Please, be careful," Irene pleaded.

He nodded and calmly made his way to the rack on the back wall, grabbed his hat and left the church.

"Let's pray," Sam said from the front. Church members exchanged looks, and then bowed their heads in prayer. "Lord, watch over our brave men, stand watch over Dr. and Mrs. Barnes and all the citizens of Jackson Springs. Protect them, Lord. Just as we sang only moments ago, You, Lord God, are their refuge and fortress. Because these good men have made You Lord of their lives, no evil shall befall them or an accident overtake them. Lord, give Your angels charge over each one this day to keep them in all their ways. We put our trust and confidence in You and ask these things in Jesus's name. Amen."

"Amen," the people echoed.

At that moment Elisabeth's concern was that Gabe had never made God Lord of his life, so she added softly, "And Lord, please protect Gabe. Keep him safe so he can one day make You his Lord and King. Satisfy him with long life as the scripture says."

The unrest in her chest eased after she'd prayed that. She was concerned for Gil, but as a believer he was probably praying right that very moment. He'd faced similar situations in the past. He was prepared for danger.

The way Gabe had avoided a confrontation on the

train that day made her surprised that he'd so willingly joined the other men at Dr. Barnes's.

"Let's break up into small groups and continue to pray," Sam suggested. The people did as he asked, forming circles and petitioning and thanking God for the safety of those who'd gone to help and those who were directly involved.

As they prayed, the sounds of gunfire reached them.

At the noise, Melissa Larken cried softly, and Josie handed Elisabeth the baby so she could comfort her. Instead of showing distress, Irene gathered all the children and took them up front near the organ, where she sat and played songs to which they could sing along. Elisabeth listened with appreciation.

Across the aisle and over several lowered heads, she met Arlene and Chess's eyes and gave them an encouraging smile. Gil knew how to take care of himself.

The door opened and closed, and she assumed someone had gone to check on the situation. A few minutes later, Karl Stone entered the building and spoke privately to Sam.

Sam glanced from face to face before saying solemnly, "Dr. Barnes has been shot. The report doesn't sound good."

Kathryn DeSmet, the schoolteacher, wept softly. Abigail and Anna hurried to her side and comforted her. Josie carried Rachel over to stand beside Arlene. Arlene automatically reached for the baby and held her close, as though doing so was a comfort and a life affirmation.

Feeling helpless, but knowing how much more difficult this was for Irene, Elisabeth guided her to a private spot.

"I can't just sit here," Irene said.

"Praying is the best we can do for them right now," Elisabeth told her.

Irene shook her head, distress evident on her face. "No. I can't take this."

She shot up and ran for the door.

Chapter Fourteen

As the dark-haired young woman ran outside, Elisabeth cautioned softly, "Irene." And then more loudly, "Irene, wait!"

Instinctively, she followed, not surprised when her father joined her in pursuit.

Irene paused for a moment, and with relief, Elisabeth realized Irene didn't know which direction would take her to the doctor's home and office. A shot rang out just then, crumbling her momentary respite. Irene gathered her skirt hem and darted toward the sound.

"Irene, come back!" Elisabeth called.

Sam was faster than Elisabeth, whose skirts impeded her progress, but Irene was faster yet, taking the lead with unexpected agility.

A grayish haze accompanied the acrid smell of gunpowder hanging in the air as they neared the house where Matthew Barnes lived and worked. Several men, including Will York and Deputy Dan Larken, crouched behind water troughs and at the corners of buildings, their guns and attention directed at the doctor's home.

Elisabeth's heart hammered at the fear that Irene was going to heedlessly run smack-dab into the center of the fray.

"Will!" her father shouted, catching the man's notice. "Stop her!"

Gil's lanky cousin shot out of his hiding place at the corner of the telegraph office and grabbed Irene around the waist.

She didn't have a chance to put up much of a fight, because at that moment another flurry of shots erupted from the house. Bullets splintered wood and kicked up jets of dust in the street. She emitted a shriek.

Sam halted and spun to grab Elisabeth's wrist and together they darted behind a building.

"Throw out your guns!" Elisabeth recognized Marshal Dalton's voice. "You're not getting out of there alive!"

"Neither are your friends," came the reply.

Elisabeth and her father moved around the back of the building which shielded them and crept up the other side so they were farther away from the fray, but could peer around the corner and watch from a closer perspective.

She spotted Gabe now, crouched behind an overturned wagon. Movement caught her eye and she discovered Gil on a rooftop, far enough behind the view from the doctor's front door and side window that no one in the house could see them. Her heart lurched. She tapped her father's shoulder and pointed. He looked where she'd directed and caught his breath.

The door to the doctor's house opened slowly inward. A patch of bright blue appeared, and as the form emerged into the sunlight, Elisabeth recognized Donetta Barnes. A man held her from behind, using her as a shield. Even from this distance, her terror was evident.

"Why is that man doing this?" Elisabeth asked around the thickness in her throat.

"Father God, keep Mrs. Barnes safe in Jesus's name," was his only reply.

Elisabeth echoed her father's prayer and leaned against him.

"Let her go!" Marshal Dalton called.

"Let us get to our horses and she might live," came the reply.

As the first man cleared the doorway and stepped off the boardwalk with his hostage, another armed man appeared behind him, holding up a third stranger who was bandaged around the waist and shoulder, his bloody shirt gaping open. The two of them were easy targets for the men in wait in every direction, but if one of them took a shot, they risked Donetta's life.

Where was Dr. Barnes? Already dead inside?

It seemed a hopeless situation either way. If someone shot the easy targets, the first man would shoot Donetta. If they held their fire and let the men escape, it was likely they'd take her along and get rid of her once she was no longer useful.

"Let her go."

Elisabeth had been so involved in her thoughts, she hadn't noticed the tall figure who now walked directly into the street, right out in the open, boldly challenging the man who held Dr. Barnes's wife in front of him. The barrel of the man's gun swung to point at Gabe.

Elisabeth's heart lurched into her throat. She was going to be sick. *Gabe!*

"What are you doing?" came Irene's distraught cry. "Gabriel, get back!"

He showed no sign that he'd heard her plea.

"I'll shoot her!" the man threatened.

"This is the last time I'm tellin' you to let her go," was Gabe's reply.

Donetta closed her eyes and remained rigid and silent in his hold. No doubt she was praying, and Elisabeth joined her by petitioning God softly enough for only her father to overhear.

All that passed were seconds, but the intense danger of the situation seemed to stretch those moments into infinity. Elisabeth couldn't imagine a good outcome. She refused to entertain visions of Gabe or Donetta shot and bleeding in the street.

The man inched away from the doctor's house, dragging Donetta with him.

More quickly than she'd have believed possible, Gabe grabbed the gun from the holster against his side and fired.

A single shot rang out and the sound volleyed against the buildings.

Both Donetta and the man holding her slumped to the ground.

Irene's scream was louder than the gunfire.

The man who'd still been standing in the doorway dropped his bandaged friend in a heap. He fired wildly at Gabe. A store window shattered. He spun and darted around the corner of the house.

Gabe ran after him.

Others moved out from behind cover with their weapons aimed at the man lying still on the ground. Donetta was sobbing, her hand at the side of her face.

Elisabeth and Sam ran toward her.

As they neared, Sam stopped her with an upheld palm. "Don't come any closer, Elisabeth."

She halted in her tracks.

Another man had joined her father, and together they extricated Donetta from the man's hold. "Where are you hit?" Sam asked.

If she was hurt badly, what would they do? Who knew what condition the doctor was in—or if he was alive at all?

"I don't think I'm hit," she said, but she wiped spattered blood from her face. Her hair was flecked with crimson.

"It's his blood," Marshal Dalton said to Sam.

Sam held Donetta steady and motioned for Elisabeth to come for her. Elisabeth couldn't resist a look at the man lying dead at their feet, and then wished she hadn't.

Donetta was trembling as Elisabeth wrapped her arm around her shoulders.

"Get her out of here," the marshal said. "We don't know if there are more inside or not."

"Three horses out back," Dan Larken told him from the corner of the house. "Accounts for these two." He gestured to the bandaged man lying in the doorway and the one Gabe had shot. "And the one he's following."

"Paul Jeffries and Voctor are watching the back, right?"

"Yeah, but there are wagons and stacks of crates. The man could hide anywhere."

"Sam, you watch this fellow. That 'un's dead. The rest of us will split up and surround the alley." He called, "Will! See if the doc's okay inside. Dan, cover him."

"I can't let go of this crazy woman," Will returned.

"You're preventin' us from doin' our jobs, little lady," the marshal hollered. "Stay put or I'll handcuff you to a lamppost."

Sam took off his belt, pinned the injured man's arms behind his back, and bound him.

Elisabeth led the sobbing woman to safety beside the building where Gabe's sister had wisely chosen to wait. Irene nearly swooned when she saw Donetta's face.

"She's not hurt," Elisabeth assured her.

"Gabe shot that man right out from behind her."

"Let's take her somewhere and clean her up."

Irene seemed to come to her senses. "Of course. What are the men doing now?"

"They're chasing that man who shot my Matthew," Donetta said. "Those swine held their guns on us and forced Matthew to tend to their friend. He had just finished wrapping his wounds when Ezra Quinn rang the bell and walked in the side door. Matthew moved toward me then, and that man shot him." Her voice broke, and she continued with a sob, "He's lying in there bleeding right now."

"The others are seeing to him," Elisabeth told her.

"I should stay," the woman said. "There's no one else who would know how to treat a wound. I'm not a doctor, but I've watched him treat a lot of injuries, bullet wounds included."

"I think she's right," Irene said.

They stood nearly a block away now, the air and the sun drying the blood smears on Donetta's face and neck. The shoulder of her blue shirtwaist was speckled red. Elisabeth spotted a neighbor peering out the second-floor window of the room she rented over a store.

"Are you all right?" Elisabeth asked. "I could leave you here and go back to help with the doctor."

"I'm fine. I want to go help Matthew."

"All right then. But we'll wait far enough back to stay out of danger until they tell us we can go in."

The three of them took the spot Will and Dan had vacated and observed the front of the Barnes's home from there. After several minutes Deputy Dan rode up beside them on his horse. "You can go tend to the doc. Your pa and Paul are taking those two to jail. The rest of us are heading out."

"Where are you going?" Irene asked. "Where's my brother?"

"He was the first one to ride out," he answered. "Took one of those men's saddled horses."

He turned his horse's head and galloped down the street, the animal's hooves kicking up dust.

Donetta jumped up and ran toward her home. The other two women followed.

The men had moved the doctor to an examination

table in his surgical office. Elisabeth took one look at the front of his shirt and then his ashen face and felt her heart drop.

Donetta calmly took a scalpel and sliced open the front of his shirt. Blood trickled from a neat hole in his chest.

"If the bullet hit his heart or an artery, trying to remove it would kill him. I don't know what I'm doing. If the bullet was somewhere else, I could do it. I don't know what to do."

"Stop the bleeding?" Elisabeth asked.

"He's been bleeding far too long," Donetta said, but she nodded. She packed the hole and applied pressure. "I don't know what to do," she said again. Elisabeth shared her sense of helplessness.

"Is there a doctor in a nearby town?" Irene asked. "We could take him there."

"Not close." Irene bent to press her lips to her husband's forehead. "The trip would likely kill him."

"We could bring the other doctor here."

Donetta met Elisabeth's eyes. "It's worth a try."

Elisabeth shot out of the house and ran all the way back to the church.

Several members still remained and, seeing her, gathered around.

"Elisabeth, are you all right?" Josie asked in alarm.

Elisabeth glanced at her hands and her Sunday dress, realizing she had come in contact with Donetta and her husband both. "I'm fine. But Dr. Barnes is hurt badly. He needs another doctor, and needs him fast."

Two men offered to ride to a nearby town for help. They left seconds later.

"What can we do?" Arlene asked.

"All of your husbands and sons are just fine," she assured them and then explained what had happened and how a posse had gone after the man who'd shot Dr. Barnes. "Continue to pray for all of them."

"I'll come with you to stay with Donetta," Arlene said and accompanied Elisabeth back to the doctor's house. Sam had locked the prisoner in a cell and returned to pray for the doctor.

The day grew warm and the afternoon stretched endlessly.

The men who'd gone after the shooter returned first, and Junie Pruitt delivered the news. The man who'd shot Dr. Barnes had returned to Jackson Springs draped over a saddle, shot to death by that Taggart fellow.

Elisabeth and Irene shared a look.

"That's two men he's killed today," Elisabeth said aloud.

"What would you have had him do?" Irene asked. "Your friend's life was in the balance." She glanced at Donetta. "Would you have wanted him to let that man ride off and get away with what he did to the doctor?"

Elisabeth shook her head. She didn't know what to think. She'd known what Gabe was capable of. She'd been there when he'd confronted half a dozen train robbers without blinking an eye. She should have read the signs then. But today, in the street...he'd shown no fear or hesitation. He'd walked directly up to a man who held a gun pointed at his chest, calmly told him to let go of the woman and then pulled his gun faster than the other man could fire. He'd shot that man right out from behind his hostage.

If she hadn't seen it with her own eyes, she wouldn't have believed such a feat was possible.

What kind of man took risks like that? What kind of man could draw and shoot as though he'd practiced his whole life for that moment?

The answer she hadn't wanted to face floated to the surface of her consciousness: *A gunfighter.*

Chapter Fifteen

Before dusk, Matthew Barnes took his last arduous breath. Donetta pressed her forehead against his and cried softly. Arlene rested her hand on the woman's shoulder to comfort her.

Tears ran down Elisabeth's cheeks, and Irene held her hand. Elisabeth wiped her face on her sleeve and stood. "Let's go ask a couple of Donetta's friends to stay with her."

The two of them exited the house and shared the devastating news with those waiting. Elisabeth located someone she knew would be a comfort and suggested the woman go on inside.

Irene learned her brother was at the marshal's office and grabbed Elisabeth's hand. "Come with me. Please."

Several men sat on the stairs and benches near the open door of the lawman's office and jail. Gabe extracted himself from their midst to join the approaching women. He looked at Elisabeth without expression, his green gaze flickering to her blood-smeared dress.

She took a shaky breath. "Dr. Barnes didn't make it."

The men behind him murmured and shook their heads. Gil ran his hand down his face and moved to stand at the edge of the boardwalk and take stock of the tree-covered mountains.

"I never want you to do anything like that again," Irene rebuked in a low angry tone. "You could have been killed. Do you think you're invincible?"

"Not with this gunshot in my side," he replied.

"Why did you *do* that?" she questioned, her tone incredulous.

He glanced from his sister to Elisabeth. Without blinking, he answered, "It's what I do."

He untethered a horse from a nearby post and led it by the reins as they walked toward their street.

"I don't want you to take a chance like that again," Irene pleaded.

"Didn't mean to frighten you. You should've stayed put at the church. Your yellin' and carryin' on lost us one gun hand when we need him."

They stood in front of the church now. Irene turned toward their little house and walked away, leaving Gabe and Elisabeth standing. The horse snorted softly behind him, and he turned to run his knuckles over the animal's forehead and nose.

It wasn't full dark yet, but a light came on in the parsonage Irene had entered. The church beside it stood dark and silent.

"She was scared," Elisabeth said softly. "We all were. Maybe you should leave her alone for a little while."

He shifted his weight. "Want a ride up the hill?" he asked.

She glanced at the horse. "I haven't ridden much."

"I won't let you fall." He hoisted himself into the saddle with a creak of leather and led the horse over to the set of steps where buggies unloaded. "Climb up."

"I don't think so." She turned and headed for home.

He followed, guiding the horse at a walk. "I'm sorry about the doc. He was a good man."

"Yes, he was."

"If there's a God, why would He let someone like that get killed?"

At that Elisabeth halted. She turned around to look up at him. "God isn't in the business of shooting people. He gave everybody free will. Free will to believe in Him or not. Free will to live for Him and do what's right or to carry guns and rob and lie and cheat. Those men chose a life without godly principles. Of course their behavior makes God sad, but He doesn't control people like puppets. We make our own choices."

"Not everyone who carries a gun lies and cheats."

"Not everyone who carries a gun kills people, either," she returned.

"Your own father has a gun. And he's a preacher."

"It's not for gunfights. It's for defense."

"Same thing."

She spun and started back up the hill.

"Your friend Gil is a deputy. You don't have a problem with that."

"But you do. You didn't want Irene getting involved with him. How hypocritical is that?"

"I don't want her to marry someone in a dangerous occupation is all. We were talkin' about you."

"Gilbert's a lawman. You're a...a gunfighter."

"I'm not a gunfighter."

"What then?"

He drew a deep breath. "Bounty hunter. But not any longer. You know I'm starting a ranch."

"Doesn't that sort of life follow you wherever you go?"

"Why don't you stop? I'll get down and we'll talk."

"We are talking."

He nudged the horse with his heels, got ahead of her and slid from the saddle to prevent her from getting past him. Gabe didn't know why it drove him crazy, but the fact that she wouldn't listen to his explanations or discuss this irritated him. He'd left one angry woman at home and was confronting another.

She leveled her gaze on him and placed her hands on her hips. "It's no business of mine what you did in the past or what you do now."

"If it makes no difference to you, why are you so mad?"

She dropped her hands to her sides. "I'm not mad. I'm...disappointed."

"I'll bet a lot of people disappoint you."

"Are you saying I'm judgmental?"

"No. Only that it's tough to live up to the standards you set for yourself and everybody else."

"They're God's standards, not mine."

He mulled that over a moment. "God doesn't want criminals brought to justice? What about that Joshua fellow your father told us the story about? He fought battles and won. What's so different about that?"

"I'm really tired, Gabe. I've had a bad day. I just want to go home."

Jaw set, he moved aside to let her pass.

She climbed the hill and he watched her reach the steep stairs that led up to the Harts' property. She didn't look back. At the top, she opened the iron gate and closed it behind her.

Why did he care what she thought of him?

He mounted his horse and led it down the hill at a gentle walk. He'd done the right thing. He'd gone after the man who'd killed Dr. Barnes and he'd caught him. That was the only justice he knew.

Most of the residents of Jackson Springs showed up for the funeral. With no family at her side, Donetta Barnes made a lonely figure in her black dress and hat. Friends and her husband's patients lent her support and sympathy.

Gabe sat with the Hart family during the church service, because Irene had immediately led him toward them. Victor Larken performed the eulogy, and then the people solemnly followed a black-draped horse and wagon along the streets to the cemetery on the outskirts of town. There Sam prayed and read from his Bible.

Gabe had witnessed more death than most people, though he hadn't attended a funeral since his parents'. Living and dying was the natural way of things.

"Let not your heart be troubled, Jesus said." Sam read, *"'Ye believe in God, believe also in me. In my*

Father's house are many mansions. If it were not so, I would have told you. I go to prepare a place for you. And if I go and prepare a place for you, I will come again and receive you unto myself, that where I am, there ye may be also.'"

These people sure set store by their Bibles. Elisabeth talked about God as though He was a real person. His sister, too, he was learning, lived by the same principles and beliefs.

"'Verily, verily, I say unto you,'" Sam continued. *"'He that believeth on me, the works that I do shall he do also, and greater works than these shall he do, because I go unto my Father. And whatsoever ye shall ask in my name, that will I do, that the Father may be glorified in the Son. If ye shall ask any thing in my name I will do it. If ye love me, keep my commandments.'"*

Gabe had heard of the golden rule, of course, and of the ten commandments. He'd figured he'd broken most of them, so what was the use in thinking God had any special love for him?

"'He that hath my commandments, and keepeth them, he it is that loveth me, and he that loveth me shall be loved of my Father.'"

Yep, he was pretty much at the end of the line in God's opinion.

"'Peace I leave with you, my peace I give unto you, not as the world giveth, give I unto you. Let not your heart be troubled, neither let it be afraid.'"

Gabe was glad if those words gave the doctor's widow some comfort. She was a real nice lady and had been kind to him during his stay at her place. But he also hoped it helped knowing the man who had taken her husband wouldn't be hurting anyone else.

He glanced aside at Elisabeth. She wouldn't understand his logic. Since he'd met her his life had become more confusing and complicated. She questioned his way of thinking. What was worse, she made him question his own thinking. She challenged him to consider things outside his realm of knowledge or understanding.

He asked himself at every turn why he should care what she said or thought. That he spent hours lying awake, going over their conversations…and their kisses should have been some kind of clue, but he still hadn't faced the truth. He'd never backed away from a confrontation in his life, but right now he was hiding from something he didn't want to acknowledge.

He had strong feelings for Elisabeth Hart. However, the timing was all wrong. Their relationship was definitely all wrong. But those facts didn't stop the way he felt about her.

He wanted to be a man she admired.

It would never happen. How could he ever measure up to her standards or the people she admired?

After a final prayer, Sam picked up a handful of dirt and handed it to Mrs. Barnes. She tossed the dirt onto the lowered coffin. Friends followed suit, the clumps hitting the wooden box until several inches of soil silenced them.

Gabe was one of the last to grab dirt and toss it into the grave. After the women and most of the people had headed back to church for a meal, Gabe joined Dan and Gil in picking up shovels and finishing the work.

"The marshal said you hunted for bounty," Gil said.

"That's right."

"Does your sister know?"

"She does now."

"And Elisabeth?"

Gabe looked up. Dan wasn't paying any attention to their conversation, but Gil looked right at him.

Gil shrugged. "I've noticed something between the two of you is all."

"She thinks I'm lower'n a snake's belly."

"Give her some time."

"Don't know if I have enough time left. She's mighty fixed on her ideas."

"You, uh…you fancy her, do you?"

"Can't sleep half the night. Can't get her out of my head."

Gil rested a hand on his hip, pausing to rest on the handle of the shovel. "A woman like that can sure get a hold on a man's thinkin', can't she?"

Gabe agreed.

"Same thing your sister does to me."

Gabe stopped shoveling to look at him. "You asking my permission or something?"

"I'd like it if you weren't opposed."

"She's every bit as set on her notions as Elisabeth. Maybe more. She wants to make her own choices and decisions about her life. A lawman's job seems dangerous to me, but look what happened to this good doctor just minding his own business. Guess there's no telling who's safe and who isn't." He tucked the shovel handle under his arm to lift his hat away from his head and tie his handkerchief around his forehead, then settle the hat back on. "If it's her choice to let you come calling, I'm not going to stand in her way."

Gil gave a satisfied nod and they resumed their grim task.

Chapter Sixteen

In the days that passed, Gabe stayed busy overseeing the construction of the house. The Barnes woman stayed on his mind. He wondered off and on how she was getting along and whether or not she would stay. If she had family elsewhere, she might join them. He remembered how alone and lost she'd seemed the day of the funeral.

Irene was content to write in her journals, perform chores around the house and accompany Elisabeth when she had notary duties. He was glad for their friendship, because he wouldn't want her stuck in that tiny house all day long.

Everything had changed now that he had feelings for Elisabeth Hart. Living in Jackson Springs was going to be difficult when he'd see her and her family—and he would, since she and Irene had developed a close friendship. Was he doomed to spend his days regretting that he would never be the sort of man she could love or marry?

But he couldn't ask Irene to leave now, not so soon

after arriving. Not when she was delighted to be here and making additional friends and feeling more at home every day.

On his way out of town early one morning, he shot a deer. After he dressed it, he took a portion of the meat to Mrs. Barnes and gave Josie the rest.

Irene hadn't caught on to cooking just yet, though she gave meals her best efforts. Some evenings they ate at the café, other nights Gabe prepared a quick meal, and when they were especially fortunate, the Harts invited them for supper. One of those evenings, the Stellings were guests as well, and Gil invited Irene to another game of checkers. Afterward, the two of them took a stroll through the gardens and sat on the porch.

He worked every day to accept this thing that was developing between his sister and the deputy. He wanted her to be happy, and if Gil made her happy, Gabe could deal with that.

Ironic how he'd always considered himself capable—invincible actually—in his line of work. He'd been solely responsible for Irene, and had something happened to him, she'd have been alone. Now in context, his concern that something could happen to the lawman was pretty hypocritical.

From all appearances his time with Irene was already running short. If she married Gil…if she married anyone…he'd be alone again. His concern was more like a father than a brother, he realized. But when it happened, he would let go.

The evening before the Independence Day celebration, Irene was beside herself with excitement when

Junie Pruitt brought her a message. Jane Carter Lockhart had arrived on the train.

Irene asked Gabe to accompany her to the hotel, where they met the famed suffragette and her husband. Gabe shook hands with the man. Funny, Gabe hadn't paid any attention to the fact that these prominent women had husbands. Attention was always focused on the woman, but he learned that Silas Lockhart campaigned right alongside his wife, petitioning for women to be able to vote in local and national elections.

The people of Jackson Springs had been preparing for the holiday for over a week, decorating the buildings along Main Street with banners and patriotic swags and constructing a platform. Even dealing with their sadness from the loss of their friend, the community moved on.

The following day Gabe stood on the boardwalk as Irene participated in the procession of decorated wagons, sharing a ride with Mr. and Mrs. Lockhart. Penelope Berry, the café owner, offered him a jar of lemonade and he enjoyed the parade from a good vantage point before returning the jar.

Abigail Hart spotted him and motioned for him to join their family. The boys greeted him as though he was one of them and Josie showed him how much the baby had grown.

Peter was sitting atop Sam's shoulders so he could see the goings-on, but John clung to his mother's skirt with a frown.

"Can I give you a seat?" Gabe asked.

Delighted, the boy raised his arms and Gabe lifted

him to his shoulders. The minimal pain the effort took was well worth the boy's delight as he watched the parade. They all shouted and cheered for Irene when the wagon she perched on slowly passed by.

He and Elisabeth had barely spoken since the evening she'd learned of his true occupation. There was nothing he could say to change her opinion of him, nor could he change who he was or what he'd done.

As the family strolled toward the booths lining the street, she glanced up at John and offered Gabe a hesitant smile. "How is the house coming along?

"Frame's up. Two fireplaces are built. Roof goes on next."

"Sounds like everything's going well. How's your side?"

"Better. Hardly notice it anymore, unless I do something without thinkin'."

"Like picking up small children?"

He shot her a glance.

"I saw you wince when you picked up John."

"He's heavier than he looks."

She smiled.

John joined his brothers then to play games along the row of booths. Eventually the band played, announcing the speeches. Gabe and the Harts joined the crowd that surrounded the platform. The mayor spoke first, expounding on the United States' freedom and the basis of this centennial celebration. He introduced the governor of the territory who spoke of their ongoing pursuit for statehood. Andrew Johnson had turned down their re-

quests for statehood, but another petition was currently
before President Grant.

After much applause for that cause, the mayor introduced Rhys Jackson. Rhys spoke about the founding of
their community and his grandfather's part in it. Eventually Irene was welcomed to the podium.

Gabe knew she'd been spending a lot of time writ-
ing, and he guessed he shouldn't have been surprised,
but when she took the podium and didn't immediately
introduce the visiting guest, he cocked his head. In a
clear voice and with heartfelt enthusiasm evident, she
spoke with knowledge and passion.

After meeting Silas Lockhart, Gabe had a more sym-
pathetic view of the suffragettes and their cause. He
caught Elisabeth watching his reactions. "I think I might
be proud of her," he said.

Spotting Gil in the crowd, he wondered about his reaction to Irene and her cause. At the moment, she held
the attention of nearly the entire town. The young man
listened intently, but he also glanced at the nearby people's faces to gauge their reactions.

"Her passion for women's rights is contagious," Elisabeth said from beside Gabe. "I've noticed only a few
grumblers in the crowd."

She drew her talk to a close and, with added excitement in her tone, Irene introduced Jane Carter Lockhart. The crowd applauded for the well-dressed woman.
She wore a jaunty hat at an angle over her upswept dark
curls.

She was indeed an impressive speaker. She incited
the gathering to applaud after every high point in her

talk. Finally, the band played and Mrs. Lockhart mingled with the townspeople, shaking hands and answering questions.

Abigail took Gabe's hand and led him to a sign-up table for the friendly competitions. "Will you be my partner at one of these? How about the three-legged race?"

"There's always the potato toss," the man at the table suggested.

"I can probably toss a potato," Gabe said.

"We need two more people for that," she told him. She glanced aside. "Elisabeth! Anna! Come join us."

The others joined them and Abigail signed them as a team. The competition began, and he discovered the snag he hadn't known about. Each person wore an apron and wasn't allowed to touch the potato with their hands. They had to use the apron to throw and catch.

"Never done this before?" Elisabeth asked as he watched.

"How can you tell? We haven't started yet."

"That frown on your face gives you away. What are you thinking?"

"I'm thinking...do people really *do this?*"

She grinned. "Some do."

He pretty much made a fool of himself, but only got hit in the shoulder with the vegetable once. In the end he and the Hart sisters took second place and congratulated each other.

Later they located the rest of the family and shared a picnic supper. As the sun lowered, ice cream makers were brought out and Gabe took a turn cranking.

Rhys Jackson spotted him. "I have a proposition for you."

"What's that?"

"I'll buy that land from you and give you one of the houses I own in town." He named a price.

Gabe mulled over the man's generous offer. What did the banker want with land so far from town? "No other spot of land you'd want?"

"I own the other pieces around that spread. Over the years I tried to find the owner of yours without any luck. If I had that section, my holdings would be joined."

"Well, you know I've taken a shine to that particular property. My house is underway. I'm not selling."

"I'll double my offer."

Taken aback, Gabe stared at him. There was something fishy about the man's insistence. "That's a tempting offer. Overly generous actually. Still not selling."

A muscle ticked in Rhys's jaw, and he thinned his lips into a straight line. "You won't get another offer like that."

"Don't want one."

The man gave him a sidelong look before moving away and joining a group of men.

Elisabeth approached with a long wooden spoon and stirred the ice cream. "That was odd."

"You heard?"

She nodded.

"Ever heard him mention looking for the owner of my land?"

"Never. Perhaps to my father."

He waited until she finished stirring and cranked again. "You're speaking to me again."

"It's rather difficult not to when my whole family thinks you're grand."

He thought a moment. "If me being around is a problem for you, Elisabeth, I'll back away and leave you be."

Her cheeks flushed pink. "That would be selfish of me. My family enjoys your company. And Irene is my friend. I don't want to make things more awkward."

"I enjoyed myself today," he said. "And I enjoyed spending time with you. Even the potato game."

"You looked awfully silly wearing the apron, but you were actually pretty good at the toss."

"Those rascals smart when they hit."

"Years past we've done it with eggs."

He raised his eyebrows. "Now that's just a waste of good eggs."

"But incentive to catch them," she replied with a laugh.

"Oh, I don't know. Not getting hit in the head with a flying potato is pretty good incentive to catch the spud. I'd still rather eat them any day."

"I've noticed."

He caught the teasing lilt to her tone. "You and your stepmother and sisters cook better than any of the cooks in the restaurants and cafés where I've eaten over the years. Only home cooking I ever had was when I was a boy. My mama was a good cook. I can still remember picking apples and her baking them into a golden-crusted pie."

"Josie taught us all to cook."

"Is she giving Irene any lessons?"

"Irene's catching on. She's a little impatient. Cooking and baking take time. You can't rush tender meat or creamy sauces. She's getting there."

"Her heart's not in it," he pointed out.

"It's not my life's ambition, either," she replied. "Some things we just do because we need to, and we might as well do a good job while we're at it."

He studied her in the fading light. Her thick blond braid hung over her shoulder, and her skin was pink from the sun and the activity. "What *is* your life's goal, Elisabeth?"

Chapter Seventeen

He'd surprised her, evident in the way she looked at him and then away. Finally she glanced back. "I'd like to use my skills in a manner that pleases God."

"Not cooking."

"Not especially. I had always wanted to go back to where I lived as a child, so after graduation I spent nearly a year back east. I studied bookkeeping."

"I didn't know that."

"I keep my father's ledgers for home and the church. I've also helped Josie with investments. She has her own money and it's set up in trust funds and stocks."

He wasn't going to ask how a young woman like Josie came by so much money, but the question nagged.

"Her father left her an inheritance, as did her first husband." Before he had a chance to consider, she explained. "She was a widow when we traveled through Nebraska and met her."

Gabe's impression of Josie Hart improved even more at the knowledge that she could have lived her life well-off and done as she pleased. Maybe traveled. Instead she'd chosen to raise a family and keep a house where the Harts could welcome friends and neighbors. What made some people so unselfish and others only out for what they could get?

"I was mean to her at first," Elisabeth admitted. "I resented her taking my mother's place in our family… and in my father's heart."

"That's understandable."

"I don't know. Abigail and Anna loved her right off. I held her at arm's length and found fault with everything she did and said."

"Maybe there's hope for me yet, huh?"

She looked him in the eye, her confusion evident. "There's no comparison."

"You're holding me at arm's length…and probably wishing your arms were longer," he said. "You don't approve of me."

"It's not the same."

"You're right. I'm sorry. What's the rest of your life goal?"

"I'm a little confused about the rest of it."

"What about children?"

"Perhaps one day. But not right now. I have plenty of children in my life."

"Not your own."

"Do you want children?" she asked.

"I suppose I do. Never thought all that much about it 'til lately, but bein' around your brothers and sisters started me thinking about family. I was so focused on setting by enough to take care of Irene and make a home for her that I didn't plan for kids of my own.

"Now I see that so much time has passed...she's already a young woman, and she'll likely be marrying and having her own family. I'm not pushing her or preventing her. She's making her own choices. It's the natural way of things should she decide she'd be happy with Gil. But then there I'd be with a big house and a ranch and no one to share it. So yeah, I guess I want kids."

He'd need a wife for that, but neither of them mentioned it.

She changed the subject entirely. "I suggested Irene join one of the footraces today, but she declined. Too undignified for a celebrity, I suppose."

"Irene?"

"Yes! You should have seen her the day of the shootings. When you left the church and she took out after you, neither Father or I could keep up with her."

"Junie Pruitt won one of the races," he said.

A couple strolled past the table where Gabe still cranked the ice cream. "Evenin', Miss Hart," the man greeted them. "Gabe."

"Evenin', Willis," Gabe replied. "You and the missus enjoyin' the celebration?"

"We've had an exhausting day, but we're staying for the fireworks." The two of them moved on.

The fellow had addressed her as Miss Hart, but Elisabeth hadn't recognized them. A lot of people knew her family because of her father's position. "Who was that?"

"Hand and his wife who work on Frank Evans's ranch."

"How do you know them?"

"I helped Willis load supplies at the mill one day. Later he showed up and lent a hand framing the house. His missus brought sandwiches and cookies for everyone that noon."

Elisabeth studied him with interest. Between her notary duties and her father's position, there weren't very many people she hadn't met at one time or another. All evening, she'd noticed him speaking to people she hadn't guessed he'd known.

"I guess it wouldn't have been proper for Mrs. Barnes to come to something like this so soon after the doc's death," he said.

"Probably not."

"And she's still dealing with her loss. Must be hard for her sitting at home with so much ruckus goin' on only a few blocks away."

"I'm sure you're right. After my mother died, it seemed wrong that life went on and people carried on with their activities, when it felt as though my life had ended."

He studied the cold confection in the freezer and stopped turning the crank. "Maybe we could take her a dish of ice cream."

Elisabeth looked at him with surprise and…an uncalled-for sense of pride. Her eyes stung at the thought of his acute thoughtfulness. She wouldn't have thought of the kind gesture. "That would be really nice, Gabe." She turned and waved to catch Arlene and Kalli's attention. The younger girl reached her first. "We're going to take some ice cream to Mrs. Barnes. Will you serve the children?"

Gabe scooped a generous portion of the dessert, and Elisabeth covered it with a red-and-white-checked napkin. "Let's hurry before it melts."

They walked the few blocks that took them away from the festivities. Seeing the doctor's home for the first time since that fateful day gave Elisabeth a sinking feeling in her stomach.

"Are you all right?" Gabe asked.

"I'm fine."

Donetta answered the door looking tired. Her dress was rumpled as though she'd slept in it. She gave each of them a once-over, followed by a tentative smile. Tucking strands of hair into the knot at the back of her head, she said, "I wasn't expecting anyone."

"We thought…well, that is, *Gabe* here thought… We brought you some ice cream."

"That's real thoughtful." Mrs. Barnes stepped back and gestured for them to enter the house.

Elisabeth handed her the bowl. "I'll get you a spoon so you can eat it before it melts." She hurried toward the kitchen.

When she returned Donetta had offered Gabe a chair in the tiny sitting room. Elisabeth handed the woman a spoon and sat beside her on the divan.

Gabe's gaze traveled to the doorway that led to the area where Dr. Barnes had treated patients.

Donetta tasted the ice cream. "This is a nice treat. People have been so kind. I have so much food I can't eat it all. And truthfully I'm not very hungry most days."

"People don't know what else to do," Elisabeth said. "And they want to help."

Mrs. Barnes glanced at Gabe. "I made a stew from the venison you brought me."

Elisabeth turned toward Gabe, who only nodded. He'd brought her meat?

"Is there anything else we can do?" he asked. "Bring wood?"

"I don't think so. I'll be moving whenever the town council finds a new doctor," she answered, and then added with a shrug, "I'm not sure just yet where I'll go."

"Seems I recall you're a fine cook," Gabe said. "You served some tasty meals when I was laid up here for a few days."

"I always cooked for Matthew and myself, of course. And I've taken meals to the jail for the past several years. I stopped doing that when one of those men responsible for Matthew's death was locked up in there."

"Think you could cook for eight or ten men?"

Elisabeth couldn't figure out what he was getting at.

"Oh, yes, easily," the woman replied.

"My sister's still learning," he told her. "But I don't expect she'll be ready to do justice to a real meal anytime soon. I'll need someone to cook for the hands. I'll have a room ready. Good-size one." He glanced around. "Probably fit in some of your favorite things."

"I don't need much," she said, her tone hopeful.

"Think about it."

"I can tell you right now it sounds like a perfect way for me to work and have somewhere to stay. We never had any children, and I don't have family."

Elisabeth slowly absorbed what had just happened. Gabe had been considering this, she suspected. He'd been thinking about Mrs. Barnes enough to wonder how she was faring on her first holiday without her husband. And he'd just found a solution for the woman's livelihood right in his own home. Just like that.

"Matthew told me you were a good man," Donetta said. "He was perceptive."

Elisabeth lowered her gaze to the bowl Donetta had placed on the nearby table and the remainder of melting ice cream.

"Thank you for helping me," she said.

"You'll be helping me out, Mrs. Barnes. You saved me from searching to hire someone. And I already know you're a good cook. The house isn't finished yet," he added. "But it will be in a few weeks."

At that Elisabeth joined the conversation. "If a new doctor is hired, you can stay with us until Gabe's house is ready."

"I'm humbled by your generosity." She had tears in her eyes now. "Both of you."

Elisabeth, too, had been humbled by Gabe's kind consideration for the widowed woman.

A few minutes later, Donetta washed the bowl, and they said their goodbyes.

"Had you been planning that?" Elisabeth asked as they walked along Main Street, where gas lamps and paper lanterns lit the booths. Another platform had been built on a grassy area beyond the businesses, and a gathering of local musicians tuned up for an evening concert. Townspeople had spread quilts and blankets and were getting children settled.

"Planned I'd need a cook is all," Gabe replied.

"How did you know she'd accept your offer?"

"I didn't." He pointed. "There's your father."

She let him change the subject, and they joined the Harts, Irene among them now. Josie had taken the baby home so the two of them could rest in the quiet house.

Irene spread an extra quilt and showed them where they could sit.

John already slept, but Peter kept jumping up and walking toward another family, where he chattered to a redheaded little girl. Sam repeatedly snagged him back and sat him on the quilt. The last time, he gave him a stern warning to stay put. The boy pouted, but crawled into his father's lap and leaned his head against his chest. Within minutes he was asleep.

The band played a selection of patriotic tunes, and when the people knew the words, they sang along.

Gabe had given Elisabeth a lot more to think about. His concern for Mrs. Barnes had been completely unexpected.

She couldn't help that she felt deceived by him. He hadn't let on that he had hunted down men for a living. He'd been evasive about his past, and for good reason.

She reached into her skirt pocket, found two smooth stones, and rubbed her fingers over their surfaces. The fact that others, like her family—and even Irene—had taken the news of his bounty hunting in stride confused her even more. She hadn't been able to forget his question when he'd asked about Joshua and the battles he'd fought, wondering how that was any different.

Perhaps Joshua fighting for his land wasn't any different from protecting Mrs. Barnes, but both were far different from setting out to chase men for the rewards on their heads. How could she look aside?

The songs turned to popular tunes of the day and old familiar music.

She felt betrayed. Deceived, plainly and simply. When she tried to fall asleep at night, she nursed that hurt. She knew dwelling on it was wrong. She'd been working to put his past out of her mind. Her resentment was a protective shell. He recognized it. She needed it there. He wasn't a man she wanted to care for.

As the band finished and the first fireworks burst overhead, Gilbert located them and joined Irene where she sat. Though the sky was dark, the fireworks created bursts of light. Elisabeth sat close enough to notice when Gilbert reached over and took Irene's hand in his.

She glanced at Gabe. He had noticed, too, but he directed his attention back to the exploding colors above. He was a handsome man, no doubt about it. She studied his profile, the shape of his nose and chin…the mouth she knew was soft.

At memories of kissing him, her resentment softened more than she liked. Anger had been her defense, but it was getting more and more difficult to stay angry. Especially when he did something like he'd done that night in offering Mrs. Barnes a position and a home.

Even if she could put his past aside—and that was a

big if—Gabe was nothing like the husband she wanted. She had expectations, and he didn't meet them. She embarrassed herself by allowing the attraction she felt and, admittedly, his kisses to veer her off her chosen path. She'd never questioned the qualities she held in esteem, still didn't. Gabe was not a man she would consider marrying.

Friendship was out of the question. She'd been friends with Gilbert for years, and their friendship was nothing like this crazy, emotionally exhausting relationship she had with Gabe. The two of them were definitely not friends.

Her head and her heart told her two different things. He might have good qualities, but Gabe didn't match up to her ideals. While fireworks burst against the black heavens and murmurs of appreciation and wonder echoed around her, she prayed for wisdom. *Lord, show me what You'd have me to do.*

She believed with all her heart that God answered prayer. She just hoped His answer came soon.

Elisabeth received a telegram requesting her services in a nearby town. She invited Irene to accompany her, but the other young woman declined. "Gil has invited me to dinner on Friday, and I need to get my good dresses aired and pressed. When do you leave?" she asked.

"Tomorrow morning."

"Will you please meet Gil with me this afternoon then? The real estate man is able to show him the Martin house at three."

Elisabeth agreed and accompanied Irene at the appropriate time. Gil and Mr. Payne were waiting on the porch when they hurried up the brick walk.

Gil greeted both of them, but his smile was for Irene. As long as she'd known him, Elisabeth had never seen him behave this way. He'd always been easygoing and polite, but he went out of his way to do things for Irene, to make her smile and to see to her comfort.

Mr. Payne let them in, and they strolled through the rooms. Eventually they reached the kitchen. "It's not yellow any longer," Gil said.

Elisabeth had noted that fact, too. "Look how big it is. And the stove comes with the house? It's a dandy."

"I don't know much about stoves," Irene commented. As the real estate man opened a pantry door and investigated, Irene said to Gil, "I'm sure someone would be able to cook fine meals in this kitchen and on this stove."

"Probably," he said.

"Now, I'm not much of a cook myself," she added.

Gilbert had said nothing about her cooking in this kitchen, but Elisabeth picked up on what she assumed came as a veiled warning on Irene's part.

Gil slanted a meaningful glance at Elisabeth. She read his plea and walked toward the back door. "Mr. Payne, will you show me the yard and outbuildings, please?"

Thomas Payne joined her quickly. "Mrs. Martin kept a fine herb garden. I'm afraid it's sadly overgrown right now."

Out of doors, she listened to Mr. Payne rattle on

about the good condition of the exterior of the home and the convenient washhouse out back. "I remember when your family moved here," he said to her. "You were just a girl when I took you and your stepmother to visit that big house on the hill. She fell in love with it right off. I couldn't believe my good fortune," he went on. "That beauty was priced head and shoulders above what most people could afford, and I figured it might take a long time to sell. But then you folks came along."

Elisabeth nodded, wondering what was going on inside while she stood out here with the real estate man.

"How is Mr. Taggart doing? I've seen him about town and he looks fit as a fiddle."

"He's good."

"Shame about Dr. Barnes, isn't it? Such a good man cut down in the prime of life. Can't help wondering what his missus will do now."

"I believe she has a job and a new home lined up."

"Well, isn't that good news? Glad to hear it."

The back door burst open, and Irene ran out, pulling Gilbert by the hand. "Elisabeth! You're the first to hear! Gil has asked me to marry him."

Elisabeth stared, surprised, though she shouldn't have been. She pressed a hand to her breast. "Oh, my goodness. Well…well, did you say yes?"

Irene laughed. "Of course I said yes."

"That's wonderful. Congratulations!"

She gave both Irene and Gil a heartfelt hug.

"None of the females in all of Jackson Springs ever caught his eye," Elisabeth said, her hand on Gil's sleeve and her statement directed at Irene. "I guess it took God bringing you right to his doorstep for him to think of marriage."

"I am a good catch," Irene said and rested her hand on his shoulder. She studied Elisabeth. "And yes, he knows exactly what he's getting into. He's duly warned that I'm not much of a cook. Between his mother and Josie, I will learn. He agrees that women should be allowed the same rights as men, and he has no intention of trying to hush me."

"I was proud of you on Independence Day," he told her.

Irene looked from his earnest face to Elisabeth and gave her a broad smile.

Elisabeth was sincerely happy for her old friend and her newest one. On one hand her head spun with how quickly this had developed. On the other, she appreciated how certain both of them had been about their feelings and the other person. Would she ever feel that way?

Of course her thoughts went directly to Gabe. She couldn't help wondering how he would react to this development. Until now she'd been a buffer for much of his dealings with his sister. She prayed he was prepared for this and that he'd be happy for her. Elisabeth expected the best.

Gilbert turned to Mr. Payne. "We're buying this house."

The remainder of the day, while Irene spoke giddily of a wedding and a honeymoon trip, Elisabeth stewed about what would happen when Gabe learned of the engagement.

"Come for supper," Josie insisted. "Gil should be here, too."

"Oh, yes," Irene answered. "We need to tell people together." Her expression changed as though she'd only just thought of something. "We'll have to tell his parents."

"After school, I'll send Anna over with an invitation to supper," Josie supplied. "Or would you rather tell them privately?"

"I'd better ask Gil about that."

"Don't worry about how they'll receive the news," Josie told her. "Arlene is one of my dearest friends, and she has already expressed her fondness for you. She is well aware that her son is completely taken with you. She'll be delighted."

"Oh, I hope so."

Josie was probably right about the Stellings. Elisabeth just wasn't as confident of Gabe. "Do we have any apples?"

"There's a bushel in the root cellar," Josie replied.

"Irene, let's bake apple pies for dessert."

"I don't know how."

"I'll show you. You can peel and slice while I make the crusts."

As the supper hour neared, the women set the table and changed into clean dresses. Elisabeth took herself outdoors to cut flowers for centerpieces.

Gunshots not far away took her by surprise. At another volley of fire, she dropped the stems and stared toward the center of town, though of course she could see nothing from here.

A bell rang, probably the one in the firehouse yard, startling her further. Another joined the peals.

Kalli ran out into the yard, the twins and Phillip on her heels. Josie followed seconds later, carrying Rachel. Abigail and Anna, who'd been reading under a tree in the side yard, abandoned their books and slates and joined them.

Josie stopped beside Elisabeth, a furrow in her brow. "What's happening?"

"I don't know."

More gunfire erupted and then a string of firecrackers and another, as though it was the Fourth of July all over again.

"I guess we'd better go see," Josie said. She turned to the younger girls. "Take the boys' hands."

As a group, they hurried down the steep brick street. At the bottom of the hill the racket grew louder. Irene was standing outside the little house, a hand shading her eyes.

Sam stood in front of the church and motioned for them to join him.

A wagon lumbered past, harnesses jingling. Several men rode in the back, waving their hats and cheering.

Sam ran forward. "What's happened?"

"The president declared Colorado a state!" one of them shouted, and the others whooped and hollered. "We have statehood!"

The men continued down the brick street, cheering and shouting the news to all who came out of doors.

Gabe rode up just then. He'd heard the reports on his way back into town. His hair was damp with sweat.

"Let's go on into town and join those celebrating," Sam suggested.

"I'll catch up with you after I wash up," Gabe replied.

The entire length of Main Street was filled with joyous citizens. One group had joined hands and danced in a circle. Others laughed and several lit firecrackers. Victor Larken carried a drum out of his store and made a racket.

Shortly, Gabe joined them. Donetta Barnes had ventured into the throng and Arlene Stelling led her over to their gathering near the post office.

At last people started home for their meals, and Josie invited Donetta to join them for supper. The widow seemed pleased to be asked. The Stellings had a buggy, so they gave Donetta and Josie a ride while the rest walked up the incline.

Gil joined them, and once they arrived at the house, Elisabeth and Josie added another place setting.

"Thank You, Lord, for answering the prayers of the people of Colorado," Sam prayed. "Lord I pray that each person in our community is thankful to You this day. Hold the citizens of Jackson Springs safe." After he asked a blessing for the food, conversation broke out. Bowls passed and there was more mirth than usual.

The voices and laughter evoked a sense of belonging and peace within Elisabeth. Sometimes she wondered how different their lives would have been if her mother had lived. But God had seen her father's need—the need of her entire family—and sent them Josie. God could take any bad situation and turn it to His glory if only His children put their trust in Him.

That situation on the train had been bad. Through it, Gabe and Irene had been welcomed into this circle of friends and family. Gil may not have found Irene if Gabe hadn't been shot and come to stay with them. And…it was difficult to think on…was God using Gabe to turn Donetta Barnes's situation around? How could that be? Didn't a person have to be willing to let God work through them?

Once everyone had finished eating, she and Kalli carried in the pies. The golden crusts and warm cinnamon smells met with sounds of appreciation.

"I helped," Irene said and gave Gil a proud smile.

"Would you like to serve?" Josie asked.

Irene stood and walked to the end of the table where the pies sat and sliced them into neat wedges. Abigail held small plates and carried the servings around the table to serve the guests first.

Gabe looked at the generous piece of pie in front of him and raised his eyes to meet Elisabeth's. She'd been thinking of him when she'd asked Josie about the apples and made the filling. Somehow he knew. He gave her a half smile that inched up his lips on one side, which in turn loosed a dozen butterflies in her stomach.

Irene squeezed Elisabeth's hand on her way back to her chair. An eternity later, everyone had eaten and been served a cup of coffee or had their milk refilled.

Finally, and Elisabeth's heart jolted with expectation, Gil cleared his throat, pushed back his chair with his legs and stood. "I have something I'd like to share with you now."

The room grew unnaturally quiet. All eyes focused on him.

The sound of the clock in the foyer could be heard over the thick silence.

He reached for Irene's hand and she gave him an adoring smile. "I can't remember being this happy." He cleared his throat again. "I've asked Irene to marry me, and she's accepted."

Arlene reached for her husband with one hand and with the other dabbed tears with her napkin. Chess held her hand and patted it, nodding with pleasure.

Gil leaned to give Irene a peck on the cheek and a quick reassuring hug. She held both his hands, gazed into his eyes and then released him to go to her brother. At her approach, Gabe inched his chair back and stood to embrace her soundly.

She leaned back and gazed up at him. "Are you happy for me?"

"I am," he replied.

"I thought you might pitch a fit when you found out."

"You buttered me up with apple pie," he said and glanced at Elisabeth.

The others chuckled.

"And besides he came to me yesterday, and we had another talk."

Irene swatted his arm playfully, hugged him again and returned to her fiancé. "Why did you let me worry?"

"I didn't know you were worried." Gil turned toward his parents. "Oh. And I bought the Martin house."

More excitement broke out. People talked over each other in their rush to share their reactions to all the day's news.

Later, after the dishes were finished and the children were in bed, the Stellings visited with her parents in the great room. Elisabeth surveyed the rooms but didn't find Irene, Gil or Gabe. She checked out of doors and discovered Gabe perched on the porch stairs by himself.

She joined him, sitting nearby and lacing her fingers over her knees. "Are you all right?"

He gazed into the star-studded heavens. "I waited too long."

Chapter Eighteen

"Too long for what?"

"To call an end to a life of chasing outlaws. To bring Irene here and make a home for her. I left her alone all those years." His voice got thick with emotion. "A child raised by strangers." He stood and walked a few feet away. "And now she's making a family for herself with no help from me, and I'm the one who's going be alone. Fitting, I suppose, because I sure don't belong with these people."

"How can you think that?" she asked. "You've already made plenty of friends since you've been here. I haven't run across anyone who didn't like you or admire you or who didn't have something good to say about you."

He shrugged. "I read people. I'm adaptable."

"You accept people for who they are," she said. "Everything's cut and dried for you. Black and white. Simple."

"People aren't that hard to figure out."

She got up to stand beside him, and with a hand at

the small of her back, he led them across the yard in the darkness.

Turning to face her, he opened his palm, and in the moonlight she recognized the stone she had given him. "You said this represents choices. Everything has a consequence, good or bad. I thought I was doing the right thing for my sister. Looking back, maybe the best school in the east wasn't the best thing I could have done for her. Maybe just knowing someone's there for you and wants you is better than all the provision in the world."

"She knows you care for her and that you only want the best for her."

"No, she doesn't. How could she?"

"Because you provided for her in the way you believed was best. She loves you, Gabe, and she believes in you."

"She believed in me all those years I was gone, too," he pointed out.

Elisabeth closed his fingers over the stone and held his hand that way. "You can't change the past. None of us can change the choices we've already made. We can only choose to make better ones in the future."

"Is that what the stones do for you? Remind you to make better choices?"

"I hope so."

"And what choice have you ever made that was so bad? You do everything perfectly."

She let his words sink in. Absorbed them. "I'm the reason my mother died."

"Didn't she drown?"

She looked away, gathering her thoughts, her composure. "Yes, she drowned. Our wagon train had come to a river. It wasn't terribly deep, but the water was swollen and running swiftly. I still get a sinking feeling when I hear the sound of a river or a bubbling stream.

"I don't know how it happened or what caused us to tip, but one moment we were all seated on the bench or just behind it, and the next moment the wagon lurched sideways, throwing my mother and Abigail and me into the water.

"The current was strong. The water was so cold it took my breath away. I was terrified, screaming, trying to swim, but my skirts were heavy. The water carried me downstream and an eddy pushed me toward a craggy bank where a limb hung out over the water. I grabbed on to it and screamed for all I was worth. I think I screamed for my mother. I cried for my father and prayed he'd reach me before I could no longer hang on."

"You must've been terrified."

"I was terrified. But I was also relatively safe, secured as I was to land by that branch. It seemed like forever I clung there, screaming until I was hoarse. And then he came. His arms locked around me, and I let go, safely carried to shore.

"Father set me down beside Anna, who had been wrapped in a blanket by one of the women from the train. Abigail was standing and her teeth were chattering so hard I thought she'd break them. Someone brought me a blanket. Eventually I stopped crying.

"I looked at Abigail. She hadn't been crying, just

watching the stretch of river beyond where we sat. 'Where's Mama?' I asked.

"'Papa's looking for her. The other men are looking for her, too.' Her lips were purple, but her face was white. I probably looked just the same." Elisabeth brought three warm stones from her pocket and looked at them. She raised her gaze to Gabe. "My mother had been carried downstream by the current. She hadn't been able to reach a branch like I had. She wasn't hanging on or safe like I had been.

"If he'd gone for her first and then come back for me—or let one of the other men fetch me—he knew I was safe—he could've reached her before it was too late."

"Did he find her body?"

She nodded. "We didn't even mark her grave. The wagons rolled right over the spot so it was indistinguishable. Like she'd never been there."

"You know they had to do that."

"I know."

"You're not responsible for her death, Elisabeth."

"Yes, I am."

"How old were you?"

"Twelve."

"How many twelve-year-olds wouldn't be frightened and calling out for help in the same situation? You had no way of knowing who was in more danger. That bank could've given way, and you'd have been buried under mud and water and not discovered. Currents like that are dangerous."

"I can't let go of the responsibility I feel," she said.

"Your expectations of yourself are unrealistic," he told her. "And so are your expectations of everyone else."

"Well, I don't think so."

"I know you don't. At least I know I'm not perfect, and I don't hope to be anytime soon."

She bristled. "I don't think I'm perfect."

"No. But you think you should be. Everyone else falls short, as well. You must wear yourself out being disappointed all the time. If something doesn't conform to your neat and tidy equation of the world, you dismiss it."

"You're just being mean now."

"Am I? Or am I being honest? You don't have a problem with telling the truth, do you?"

"How did this conversation get twisted around to be about me?" she asked. "We were talking about your sister." His accusations stung. She had shared her most private feelings with him, which she now regretted with all her heart.

"I'm traveling in the morning," she said. "I'm going to bed." With that, she turned and hurried back to the house.

Once everyone said their good-nights, Gabe ushered Irene home. She was happy, and he would never say or do anything to tarnish her tender feelings or discourage her from seeking the life she desired. After getting them both a pitcher of water, she wished him a goodnight and ducked into her tiny bedroom.

Gabe washed and lay atop the covers, staring at the

shadows of the oaks dancing on the ceiling. Half an hour later, he got up and walked quietly out into the kitchen and dipped fresh water to drink. He lit a lantern and sat in one of the two chairs at the tiny table. A leather-bound book rested within reach. He pulled it toward him and opened it.

The pages were thinner than in most books, the text in columns. He recognized Irene's Bible and turned to a few of the pages marked with slips of paper.

Proverbs caught his attention and he read several, then flipped back and found Psalms. He ran his finger over a few verses. If he hoped to gain any understanding, he'd better go to the beginning of this chapter.

There was a lot of talk of the law and the ungodly and heathen and kings. But as he read forward the writer cried out for God to save him and hear his cries.

In chapter seven, he lingered over the words of the psalmist. *The Lord shall judge the people. Judge me, O Lord, according to my righteousness, and according to mine integrity that is in me.*

Gabe sure didn't want to be judged on his actions or his decisions. It gave him some peace of mind to think that God would judge him according to his integrity. He knew right from wrong, and he had upheld what he believed was right by seeing that those who'd murdered and stolen came to justice. Whenever it had been possible, he'd brought that person back to sit in court before a judge. Killing had always been a last resort.

Further on he read that the heathen are sunk down in their own pits and the wicked are snared by the work of their own hands. Their choices to do wrong had caused those men he'd hunted their own fates.

He wanted to know more about that Joshua fellow Sam had talked about. How in this whole fat book of names and places would he ever hope to find the one?

On one of the first pages, he found a table of contents and ran his finger down the names of the chapters. Come to find out, Joshua had his own chapter.

Gabe extinguished the lantern and carried the book back to his room. Irene wouldn't mind if he borrowed it.

A couple of weeks later, Gabe stood inside the bank, securing a cashier's check.

"You've been having a lot of expenses," Rhys said, coming out of his office.

"Nothing comes free," Gabe replied.

"My offer still stands for the land."

"Still not interested. The house is almost finished. I'm heading for Durango to buy horses first thing in the morning."

"Got riders to help you with that?"

"Hired two cowboys a week ago. They're workin' out just fine." He tucked the check inside his vest pocket and left.

Elisabeth exited the courthouse after witnessing a legal transaction. Tying the ribbons of her bonnet under her chin, she spotted Gabe mounting his horse in front of the bank.

Since the night of Irene and Gil's announcement, he'd accepted Josie's invitations to dinner and had been cordial to Elisabeth, but they'd barely spoken. He was busy getting his ranch established, and she was…well, she was busy, too.

August drew to a close, and September was still warm, but the nights were cold. Elisabeth helped Josie launder bedding and quilts and hang them in the morning sun.

"I sense you're holding some things inside lately," her stepmother said to her. "You're not yourself."

Elisabeth waved the skirt of her wet apron in hopes of drying the fabric more quickly. "I've had a lot to think about."

"Do you want to talk about it?"

Elisabeth thought a moment. "I'm not ready."

"I understand you're a very private person, Elisabeth. And your feelings run deep. But don't hold things in that your family could help you with."

Elisabeth nodded. She appreciated her stepmother's concern and her wise counsel, but she wasn't ready to voice her feelings.

"You know, my favorite place to go think has always been up the mountainside. Once you get about a third of the way up this incline behind the house, there's a deer trail that leads to the most beautiful scenery you can imagine. You can look over the treetops and streets of Jackson Springs and to the south, the valley and ridges." She glanced that direction now. "It seems silly, but I've never shared my place with anyone before. It's my refuge."

"Like our turret room," Elisabeth said.

"But more private because I've been the only one

to ever go there. It's a good place to feel close to God and to think," she said. "In case you should ever want to walk up there and be alone, I just thought I'd let you know."

Josie's secret place intrigued her, and the idea of investigating it stayed with her. Once the laundry was dry and the beds made with fresh sheets and the winter quilts, Elisabeth changed her clothes, picked up her Bible and made her way up the mountainside. The deer trail was easy to find, and she followed it until she came out at the place Josie had described.

There was no mistaking the location. She could see for miles in one direction, and in the other look down at the tops of homes and see the square yards, outhouses and clotheslines. She recognized trees in rows that obviously lined streets. Smoke curled from chimneys, and she picked up the faint smells of burning wood and coal. Farther up, above the ridge, the aspens were turning gold.

She imagined Josie as a newcomer to this town, newly married to a man she barely knew, faced with three young girls who had lost their mother—one of them being downright rude to her—and could see how this vantage point had been a refuge. From here the entire world appeared small and insignificant. Elisabeth felt small, but also like a part of something bigger than herself and infinitely more important than her day-to-day concerns.

God cared about her every need, she never doubted that. But His majesty and power became very real when gazing upon the beauty and magnificence of His creation. A scripture came to mind, and she said aloud, "Who am I, Lord, that You are mindful of me?"

She sat on a flat outcropping of rock and opened her Bible to the Psalms, quickly turning pages. *When I consider the heavens and the work of Thy fingers, the moon and the stars, which Thou hast ordained, what is man that thou art mindful of him?*

She knew precisely how David had felt, awed as he was by God's magnificence. She read all of Psalm eight twice, and then traveled back to the preceding chapter and read. *Oh, Lord my God, in Thee do I put my trust: save me from all them that persecute me, and deliver me.* She read on. *Arise, Oh, Lord, in Thine anger, lift up thyself because of the rage of mine enemies, and awake for me to the judgment that Thou hast commanded.*

The Lord shall judge the people. Judge me, Oh, Lord, according to my righteousness, and according to mine integrity that is in me. Oh, let the wickedness of the wicked come to an end, but establish the just. For the righteous God trieth the hearts and reins. My defense is of God, which saveth the upright in heart. God judgeth the righteous, and God is angry with the wicked every day. If he turn not, he will whet his sword. He hath bent his bow and made it ready.... His mischief shall return upon his own head, and his violent dealing shall come down upon his own pate.

Elisabeth read these verses with a new perspective. Obviously God didn't approve of people who did wicked things, but these were strong words. Words of warning and judgment. God ordained his arrows against the persecutors! Men like Goliath who tormented the king's army? He had fallen to a young boy's stone. Men like the one who killed Dr. Barnes?

"Thank You for showing this to me, Lord." She read aloud the last verse in the Psalm. "'I will praise the Lord according to His righteousness, and will sing praise to the name of the Lord most high.'"

Even a preacher's daughter had to work things through on occasion. And yes, maybe she was as hard on herself as Gabe claimed. But much was expected of her—from God, from her father, from the community.

She'd been as disturbed by the fact that Gabe had hidden his profession from her as she'd been by the occupation itself. Looking at it from his point of view she could see where he'd wanted to start over and not carry the baggage of his past into a new life.

Humming a little, she admired the expanse of blue sky and the various green hues of the trees. Eventually she made her way back down the hillside. Instead of going into the house, she traveled down the street to the church and entered through the side door.

Pausing outside her father's office, she rapped softly on the open door. He looked up from the papers and his Bible spread across his desk. "I didn't expect you today. I thought you were helping Josie."

"We're finished with the laundry. I even had some time to go off by myself and think."

"You don't do that often enough."

"I probably need to, don't I?" She sat on one of the chairs in front of his desk. Sometimes she sat there when they discussed sermon topics and on occasion she stopped to visit, but today she felt like one of his parishioners who'd come for counsel.

He rested his ink pen in its holder and flattened both hands on his paperwork. "What's on your mind, daughter?"

Chapter Nineteen

"Were you disappointed when you learned what Gabe had done before coming here?"

"I wasn't awfully surprised," he replied. "Not after hearing how he handled those train robbers and seeing how he walked right up to that man who was holding Donetta Barnes. I can't really say I was disappointed. The elements simply fell into place and made sense." He studied her. "I take it you were disappointed?"

She admitted she was. "I understand that plenty of men carry guns," she said. "But you carry yours for protection. You don't set out in the morning to shoot someone."

"What about Gil?" he mentioned. "His gun is for protection, but also to uphold the law if need be. He doesn't go to work in the morning planning to shoot someone. And I doubt that's how Gabe set out to bring in criminals."

"I'm sure you're right."

He studied her a moment longer. "He wasn't judging the people he tracked down. Either they'd already been judged by a court and found guilty or he planned to turn them over to the law and a judge once they were in his custody."

"But he did shoot men. And kill them."

"Yes."

She'd probably thought about this too much, but she couldn't let it go. "Couldn't he just shoot them in the knee or something?"

"Have you asked him that?"

She shook her head. "No."

"How effective do you think that would have been with Mrs. Barnes's life at stake?"

"That was different."

"They were probably all different," he suggested. "Each one an individual case with its own degrees of danger and difficulty. Ask him if a shot in the knee was ever good enough."

"All right."

"David was the apple of God's eyes, and he killed men in battle. However unpleasant Gabe's work was, he did a service to protect law-abiding citizens. Someone has to do that job or the country would be overrun with outlaws."

She begrudgingly acknowledged the truth of his statement with a nod.

"You asked me how I feel about him. I can only guess how you feel about him, but ask yourself this— What does God feel toward Mr. Taggart?"

She looked at her father with surprise.

"Well?" he asked.

"God loves him," she answered.

"And places great value on him," he added.

And with that, Elisabeth had even more to consider. She got up and skirted around the desk to give her father a peck on the cheek. "Thank you."

"Who's coming for dinner tonight?" he asked.

"No one that I know of."

"Ah, an intimate family dinner." He chuckled. "See you then."

Out of doors, she strolled toward the corner. Irene called to her, "Wait, Elisabeth! I need to ask you something."

She paused and waited for Irene to join her near the curb.

"I'm planning to take the train to Denver and shop for a wedding dress. Would you like to come with me?"

Elisabeth could think of half a dozen reasons not to accompany her, but knowing how important the trip was to Irene, she said, "I'd love to go with you."

Irene beamed and hugged her. "Oh, thank you. We'll have such fun. Maybe we'll go to the theater while we're there."

That evening after supper while the family was occupied with their individual activities, Elisabeth again made the trip down the hill. She knocked on the door of the parsonage, relieved when Gabe opened the door.

"Irene isn't here."

"I suspected as much. I was hoping to speak with you."

He glanced over his shoulder, and then stepped outside. "Want to walk?"

"All right."

He went back in and returned wearing his vest, so she knew he'd gone back for his ever-present holster. They walked slowly toward the central portion of town, passing home after home with lights glowing behind windows.

"What's on your mind?" he asked.

"I've been doing a lot of thinking," she answered. "Today I spoke with my father, and he had more insight into some of the things that have been troubling me."

"He's a wise person."

"Yes, he is."

"Good listener," he added.

That remark had her wondering. "Have you…talked to him about personal things?"

"Some."

She couldn't fathom it. But of course her father wouldn't speak of it to her. Neither would he share their private conversations with Gabe or anyone else. "You surprise me at every turn."

"What's so surprising?"

Every time they had a conversation, it got off track, and she wasn't going to let that happen this time. "Nothing. What I wanted to mention to you was that he suggested I ask you about some of the things I was wondering, rather than just letting my thoughts run rampant."

"What do you want to ask?"

"It's about your occupation. Regarding what you did before you came here."

"Hunting for bounty, Elisabeth. Go ahead and say it."

"Bounty hunting," she punctuated with a nod. "Where did you travel?"

"Wherever an outlaw's trail led me. I've sought men everywhere from the Dakota Territories to the lower half of Texas."

"How did you know who to look for and where they'd be?"

"Well…there are a couple of agencies who send out papers on wanted men. They pay higher bounties than local towns or state law enforcement agencies. Most every town has a marshal or a sheriff's office, and the bigger ones keep the up-to-date papers.

"As for where to look, well, knowin' that takes a lot of footwork and talking to the right people. Nobody can disappear, though, it's a fact. And people like to talk."

"I'm sure you had to be careful, because once the person you were seeking found out you were after him, he would try to kill you before you got to him."

"That's the truth."

"And when you did find a man…say for example he'd changed his name and his ways and settled down, perhaps even had a family. What did you do then?"

"I didn't go busting into their house and shoot 'im at the dinner table if that's what you're asking. I waited to find him alone, got the jump on him and handcuffed him. Most fellas like that went along peaceable like."

"And the others? The ones who were still robbing trains and what have you?"

"I still got the jump on them and tried to take them in without a fight."

"I guess some fought back. Or ran."

"Some." He paused just as they reached the trumpet-vine-covered arbor that led into the midtown park. "If you want to know how many men I killed, I can't tell you that. I didn't keep a log or notch my belt. Sometimes it happened, just like it happened that day in front of the doc's place."

"Did you…did you ever aim so as not to kill them if you could help it?"

"Yes."

They entered the park, which was lit only by two gas lamps at the entrance. Elisabeth knew the layout, so she led the way to a center area with stone benches.

They sat. The stones under them were still warm from the day's sun, and the heat felt good since the night air had cooled.

"If it makes you feel any better, Irene asked me some of the same questions."

That did make her feel a little better.

"Did you learn all you wanted to know?"

"Thank you, Gabe. Yes."

"Since we're talking, I have a question for you."

"All right."

"Weeks ago, when we first spoke about Gil and Irene, and I asked if you had feelings for him. Then I asked you about Rhys and you said—I can't remember your exact words—but you said you weren't in the market for a husband, unless God sent you one."

"That's still true," she said.

"I asked then how you would know. You said we'd talk about it later, but you never answered my question.

So I'm asking again. How will you know if God sends you a husband?"

She had to think about it. How *would* she know? "If I even suspected, I would pray about it," she began.

"And what would you ask God for?"

"I'd ask Him to give me wisdom." She'd done that actually. "And I'd ask Him to point me in the direction He'd have me to go. And I'd ask for my will to become His."

"Pray for wisdom," he repeated. "How would you know if you got it?"

"There's a book of the Bible called James, and James says if any of us lacks wisdom, we should ask God and He'll give it to us. So we only have to ask, and wisdom is ours."

"I know who James is," he said. "And I know his book is toward the back."

She stared in surprise. "Yes!"

"I started reading Irene's Bible one night. A day or so later she bought me my own."

"She never said anything."

His shrug was barely perceptible in the semi-darkness. "And after those prayers, then what?"

"Then I'd be open to direction. It's not easy to explain."

"Try."

"For me, when I question whether or not something is right for me…if I have doubt, that's probably a sign to back off. When it's right—for example the job I took as the notary, I was at peace with the idea from the start."

"I've tracked a lot of outlaws who were probably at peace, but doing wrong."

"I doubt they truly had any peace, and if they weren't convicted of their wrongdoing, it was because they had neglected the little voice inside for so long that they'd become immune to a sense of right and wrong. The Bible talks about hardened hearts."

"You were right not to answer me that night, even if you didn't know it," he told her. "I wouldn't have understood your replies."

"That wasn't why I avoided the question." She wanted to see him more clearly, so she scooted closer to where he sat. "And now you do understand?"

"I think so. Irene prayed for me all the years I was gone. Your father prayed for me when I was shot. I wonder...have you ever prayed for me?"

"Yes," she replied. "The day you walked out there in front of that man with the gun. I prayed for God to keep you safe so that one day you'd know Him as Lord."

"And He kept me safe."

"Yes."

"What else have you prayed about?"

"I've been confused a lot, so I've prayed for wisdom."

"I guess you got it since it was promised to you."

"I guess I did. I did figure out some of the questions I had. And I was wise enough to listen to my father and ask you about my concerns."

"There's a lot about me that bothers you. I scare you."

Yes, admittedly he did. Or perhaps it was more her reactions to him that frightened her.

"I make you feel things you don't want to feel."

Maybe that was so.

"If you let go of all the anger and disapproval and let yourself feel, that would frighten you, too. If you felt anything for me—or for anyone—it would challenge your thinking."

"I'm working on letting go, Gabe."

"Maybe you're afraid of losing your freedom."

"I don't believe that thought scares me," she told him. "I'm seeing how Irene and Gil are handling that, and as long as a husband was open to me keeping my notary job and still helping my father, marriage wouldn't inhibit me."

"You don't want children. That might hold you back."

"I didn't say never. I just said not right away."

"It's just me then. I scare you."

"I'm not afraid of you."

"But you're afraid of loving me."

Chapter Twenty

Her heart stopped. Discussing anything with him became impossible because he was so deliberately challenging. "Why do you have to do that?"

"What?"

"I'm trying to work through things in my head, hold civil conversations, and you add more confusion."

"You came looking for me this time." He got up and paced a few feet away. "You wanted to talk."

"I do want to talk."

"Maybe you do too much talking and too much thinking and not enough feeling," he said. "Our discussions never end well." He walked back to stand in front of her and reached for her hand.

She offered it and he pulled her to her feet and into his arms. She steadied herself with a hand on his solid arm. Standing so close she could smell the starch in his shirt and the soap he'd used.

"Here's something we agree on." He lowered his head and pressed his lips to hers.

If only life and relationships were as simple as a few

nice kisses, she thought. If kissing him was the only thing she had to concern herself with, he was right—they could get along.

He released her, took her hand, and led her back in the direction from which they'd come. "I hear you're going to Denver with Irene," he said.

"Yes. We're staying over at least one night. Maybe two."

"I was hoping you'd agree to do some shopping for me while you're there."

"What is it you need?"

"A stove, table and things for the kitchen. Do you know how to select things like that?"

"I could figure it out," she replied.

"And furniture," he added. "At least three beds and bureaus, and a few chairs and whatever else a house needs."

That was a lot of responsibility. "Are you sure you don't want to choose those things yourself?"

"I'd grab whatever I saw first. You, on the other hand, will compare prices and sizes and concern yourself with colors and the like. You'll do a much better job."

She found it noteworthy that he had her pegged so accurately. "Do you have a budget?"

"I've had money wired to the bank there. I'll give you the papers, and you can withdraw it as you need it. I trust you to be frugal and yet purchase things of quality."

"I'd enjoy shopping for those things. But I need you to be a little more specific. Do you have a floor plan of the house?"

"I could bring it up tomorrow evening so we could go over the rooms."

"All right. I'd feel more confident with better knowledge of what it is you need."

"One more thing I'm indebted to you for."

"You're not indebted to me."

"I have no way of repaying how you and Josie took care of me when I was laid up, or for all the meals…or for taking Irene under your wings."

"There's no tally for kindness, Gabe. If a person expects something in return for a good deed, he shouldn't do it."

They'd reached the street and walked past darkened buildings into the neighborhood until they reached the church. "I'll walk you up the hill," he told her.

"It never crossed our minds how many times we'd be walking up this hill when we picked out our house," she told him. "Josie bought it as a surprise for my father."

"I'll bet he was really surprised."

"Yes." She looked up at him. "Especially because she'd never mentioned she was wealthy before they were married, and he had no idea."

"There are definitely worse things to learn about the person you married."

They laughed together. The moment felt right. She was glad she'd come right out and asked the things she'd been wondering about. He'd been straightforward about all if it, even asked her about something he'd had on his mind. Elisabeth felt as though they had shared something special as only friends could do. Maybe she'd been wrong. Maybe she and Gabe could be friends.

* * *

The Jacksons were their guests for supper the following evening. Beatrice told Sam how much she was looking forward to fall and the cooler temperatures.

"The nights have been perfect for sleeping," Sam mentioned.

"Perhaps I'll find that out sometime soon," Josie added.

Sam gave his wife an apologetic look. "Little Rachel would rather be awake during the night than during the day."

"I remember Rhys went though that stage, too," Beatrice said. "And his father slept right through the racket."

Rhys gave his mother a sidelong glance. "I'm sure he had to get up and go to work at the bank in the morning."

"You're right, he did," she answered. "And there's nothing the father can do when that little one is hungry."

Rhys kept his eyes on his plate.

Eventually, the meal was over and Elisabeth sent Josie to join their guests while she and her sisters did the dishes. She was drying a stack of plates when Gabe showed up in the kitchen doorway.

"Your father offered me a seat in the great room, but I told him I'd come to see you."

"Did you have supper?" she asked.

He nodded, but his gaze slid to the peach cobbler at the end of the work table.

Elisabeth spooned out a generous serving, poured

cream over the top and sat it along with a spoon on the table. "The coffee is nearly ready. I'll pour you a cup when it's done."

He sat. "Did you make this?"

"Abigail did. She's the best baker of the three of us."

Gabe tasted a spoonful. "This is the best peach cobbler I've ever tasted," he told Elisabeth's sister.

Abigail gave him a warm smile. "Thank you, Mr. Taggart."

"How old are you? Twenty? Thirty-five?"

She giggled. "I'm seventeen."

"Well, I envy the people you'll be cooking for when you're twenty-five."

"That will be my husband and all of my children," she said. "I'm going to have a big family, just like Papa and Josie. And a house like this one, with lots of room for guests."

"That's a good plan," Gabe told her with a wink. "Is there anyone special you have your eye on now?"

"I used to like Lester Quinn, but he has poor table manners. James Finley was sweet on me in elementary school, but his family moved to Idaho."

"I guess you'll know when God brings you a man to be your husband, won't you?" Gabe suggested.

"I guess I will." Abigail got a cup and poured him coffee. "I just hope he has good table manners."

Gabe and Elisabeth exchanged an amused look while she mulled the fact that he'd just mentioned God in a matter-of-fact way. As though he'd changed his thinking on the subject. She'd noticed he was a good listener, and he asked questions as though he was genuinely interested in others. He had the uncanny ability to draw things from them that she'd never heard before. "God knows your heart," Elisabeth said to her sister. "And He'll send you a husband who is right for you. If the fellow has poor manners, you'll just have to overlook that or give him lessons in etiquette."

"I won't be overlooking it," Abigail assured her.

"What if he's as handsome as a prince?" Gabe asked.

"Charm is deceptive, and beauty is fleeting," she replied.

"Proverbs?" he questioned.

She nodded.

"What if he's as rich as a king?"

"Better that he's wise," Abigail replied. "Solomon asked for wisdom, and because he didn't ask God for riches, he got wisdom, plus riches and honor. He was the wisest man who ever lived, you know."

"No one's ever going to best a Hart sister in a battle of wits," he said with a shake of his head. "You have a good plan. Don't let anything shake you from it. Are you sure you're not thirty-five?"

Abigail laughed.

"As long as I eat with good manners, will you keep making these delicious cobblers? I will even plant fruit trees on my land just for you."

Her smile lit up her face. "You will? Can I come pick fruit? What? Cherries and peaches?"

"Whatever you like. And you're welcome anytime.

You can bring all of your children, too, and I'll teach them to ride."

Abigail glanced at her older sister. "What about Elisabeth and her children?"

"They're welcome, too. What shall I plant for you, Elisabeth?"

She hung a towel to dry and removed her apron. "How long does it take chestnut trees to mature and produce nuts? I do enjoy chestnuts in stuffing at Thanksgiving."

"I'll look into that."

She sat at the table. "Did you bring a floor plan?"

He reached into his vest pocket and withdrew a paper that he unfolded and spread on the table. "I drew this for you. The measurements are pretty accurate. You can get an idea of room sizes and what we'll need."

"Is this a dining room?"

"It is."

"Do you want furniture for that right away?"

"It can wait if you don't want to bother, but if you see something like what's in your parents' home, buy it."

"A table and chairs, a sideboard…even a china cabinet?"

"I guess I'll need dishes, right?"

She looked at the sketch. "The kitchen seems plenty big enough for a table. You'll be feeding ranch hands every night, right?"

He nodded.

"I'd get a long narrow table for the kitchen. That way they can wash up outside and come in through the rear door—here—and it would be a lot easier for Mrs.

Barnes to serve and clean up from there than carrying it all into another room.

"You will want to furnish your dining room, but I'd wait on that until you have the rest of the house service-able and ready for work."

"You got that wisdom already," he said.

She met his eyes, and he was smiling at her in that way that lifted one side of his mouth and curled her toes. "I'm inordinately practical," she informed him. "Always have been."

"That's why I trust you to do this."

"I'll do the best I can."

"I know you will."

Abigail had left the room while they were talking, leaving them alone.

He covered her hand with his, his calluses grazing her knuckles and sending a shiver up her arm. "What you feel for me isn't practical, is it?"

"Not in the least."

"Your father and Josie, they have a practical mar-riage?"

"He needed a wife. She was widowed and wanted a family. That was practical."

"I guess it worked out well for them," he said.

"I guess it did."

"Not everything in life is practical," he suggested.

He glanced at her as though assessing her. Her hair was in a practical braid so it didn't get in the way during the day. Her clothing was plain and unremarkable. What was he thinking when he studied her?

He reached for the chain above her collar and gently

extricated the wedding ring from under the top of her shirtwaist so that it hung atop her clothing. "That's not practical."

"It's sentimental," she replied.

"Do you own anything that's just for fun?"

After thinking, she shook her head.

"You wore ribbons in your hair to church," he said. "And your straw hat has little painted cherries with paper leaves."

She widened her eyes. He remembered the details of her clothing and accessories?

"They're not necessary. But do they make you happy?"

"I suppose so."

"I could make you happy if you'd let me."

His words set her nerves on edge.

"Remember how much fun we had together on Independence Day?"

"Life isn't all ice cream and fireworks," she told him.

"Isn't life whatever you make it?" he asked.

"We need to talk about the furniture," she insisted. "If I'm going to do this, I need to be completely knowledgeable about your needs."

He released her hand. "Yes. Let's talk about the shopping trip."

She had to force herself to listen, because his insistent flirting knocked her off-kilter, as usual. The man was full of surprises. She'd been pretty sure she had him figured out, but the more she learned, the more she realized she didn't know him at all.

He'd teased Abigail in a brotherly manner, while at the same time encouraging her dreams of the future. He'd been responding knowledgeably to Biblical references, indicating he'd been reading the Bible Irene had given him. Elisabeth tried to picture it, but couldn't.

Nursing her sense of betrayal regarding him not telling her he was a bounty hunter was making her feel smaller and smaller. He hadn't lied, though not being forthright was the same. He'd explained himself whenever asked. His job had been to uphold the law, and he'd done it the only way that worked out here in this part of the country.

She remembered her father's comment about society needing men like Gabe or else the country would be overrun with outlaws, and she supposed that was true.

But even if she could set all that aside, he still didn't meet the standards that she'd already set for a husband. He was nothing like her father. He'd never been to church before he got here...never read a Bible. He didn't even have a basic knowledge or know about people in the scriptures.

Maybe she did have cherries on her hat, but she'd have a different hat come winter.

Shopping for her wedding dress in Denver, Irene wore Elisabeth to a frazzle. Nothing suited her, but finally on the second day they stumbled upon a seamstress with stunning dresses on display. The woman agreed to make her a dress just the way she wanted it and took numerous measurements.

"What about you, miss?" the woman said to Elisabeth. "You'll need a dress for the wedding, won't you?"

"Oh, goodness, yes!" Irene's eyes shone with excitement. "You'll stand up with me, won't you?"

"Me?"

"Who else? You're my dearest friend. Any friends I had at the academy have been scattered to the winds. Besides, those weren't friendships like ours. Say you will, Elisabeth."

"Of course," she agreed.

"What color?" the seamstress asked.

"I'd love it if she wore pale blue," Irene said. "Don't you think it would be a good color for her? And I will add pale blue ribbons to my bouquet and to the flower arrangements at the church."

"I have just the fabric," the woman said and rushed toward her store room, returning with a bolt of the most beautiful cloudlike blue chiffon Elisabeth had ever seen. "Will this be too insubstantial for a fall wedding?"

"The days are warm," Elisabeth assured her. "But the nights are considerably cooler."

"We'll make you a white fur wrap for evening," the woman suggested. "Like this one." She showed the two young women a soft white rabbit fur stole.

"Do you like it?" Irene asked.

"I like it a lot actually."

The seamstress measured Elisabeth. "I can make a hair bob with matching white fur, rhinestones and pieces of the dress fabric." She turned to Irene. "Can you ladies come back in two weeks for an initial fitting?

I want to make certain the basic dresses are perfect before we start adding lace and beads and trim."

"Will you be able to return with me?" Irene asked Elisabeth.

"Yes, of course. I'll probably need to finish your brother's shopping anyway."

Irene accompanied her on a hunt for a stove. Once that was selected and purchased, Elisabeth had a driver take them to each one of the furniture makers so that she'd seen every last available piece before making a decision.

"Help me choose bedroom furniture," she said to Irene. "The less ornate pieces appeal to me, but perhaps your brother would like something fancier."

"I agree on the more simple pieces. The other parts of the rooms, like curtains and coverlets, can always be added and changed."

"We didn't talk about this, but each room needs a rug. Floors are awfully cold come December and January."

Irene pointed across the street. "I saw carpets in the window over there."

With Irene's help, Elisabeth selected three sets of bedroom furniture and six room-size rugs. They made a trip to the bank, and she returned to each store to pay for all the items and plan their delivery.

"The other things are going to have to wait until tomorrow," she told Irene. "We have plans for the theater tonight."

Relieved, Irene smiled and hugged her. "Let's start getting ready and have an early dinner."

Two hours later, as the carriage they'd hired drew closer to an enormous two-story brick building, Elisabeth noted that the entire front was larger and square, a facade for the slant-roofed long narrow building behind it.

As they pulled directly in front, light spilled from the windows on the first floor and loud music met their ears. Both women stared out the windows in confusion.

The carriage jostled as the driver climbed down. He opened the door.

Elisabeth accepted his assistance and climbed to the ground. "Are you sure this is the right place?"

"You wanted the Denver Theater, didn't you, miss?"

"Yes, but this…this doesn't look like a theater."

"The performances actually take place on the second story. The entrance is on the side over there. This first floor here is a saloon and gambling hall. You can try your luck at any number of games. Faro, poker, roulette, monte, chuck-a-luck…and you don't have to worry about your play getting over too late. The place is open twenty-four hours a day, seven days a week."

Dubious about the wisdom of being left in front of this establishment, Elisabeth turned to Irene, who now stood beside her. The other young woman wore a concerned frown.

"Need a hand, ladies?" A burly fellow in wrinkled trousers with suspenders over his flannel shirt called to them. "I'd be glad to show you around. Appears to me you're new to the gaming tables."

"We were just leaving, thank you." Elisabeth turned.

"Back in," she said to Irene. "Please return us to our hotel."

"Elisabeth," Irene whispered and grabbed her arm. She was staring over Elisabeth's shoulder toward the noisy gambling hall. "Isn't that…?"

Elisabeth followed her gaze. At the corner of the building, a gas lamp shone down on a gathering of well-dressed men. "Rhys?"

Chapter Twenty-One

"That's what I thought."

"Maybe he's here for the theater." Once they were back inside, before the driver shut the door, she asked, "Wait just a few minutes, please. Until that group of gentlemen over there moves along." She leaned back to stay out of view and still be able to see.

The driver climbed back atop the carriage.

One of the men shook hands with Rhys before turning and leaving. The rest of them, Rhys included, walked to the front door and entered the hall.

Apparently the driver had been watching, because the carriage pulled away from the curb.

"Sorry about our evening plans being spoiled," Irene said.

"We'll go to the music hall tomorrow evening," Elisabeth suggested. "I've been there before, and it's not located over a saloon."

They laughed together.

"Will you tell your father?" Irene asked. "That you saw Mr. Jackson there?"

"I'm not sure what I should do." And she didn't. The Jacksons had been guests at their table for the past seven years. Elisabeth perceived that Rhys would have welcomed her interest and, because he was such a close friend of the family, she had considered the idea of courting. She wanted to give the man the benefit of the doubt, but seeing him at that place didn't really leave much doubt.

"Yes, I'll mention it to my father," she decided. "Then he'll have as much information as I do and can form his own opinion."

The following morning they finished shopping for furniture and household wares. Most of the afternoon was spent looking for slippers and underclothing. Elisabeth let Irene know she'd need boots and a warm coat in the coming months, so that was next on their list of errands. Elisabeth sent telegrams to her father and Gabe informing them the two of them would be staying a second night.

They enjoyed a leisurely supper and attended the music hall before spending their last night at the hotel.

Gabe and Gil met them at the train station the following day.

Gil swept Irene up in a hug and spun her in a circle. "I sure missed you."

Standing right there on the platform with passengers moving around them, she tipped her head back and kissed him.

Elisabeth glanced at Gabe just as he looked at her. He gave her a grin.

"Did you notice I was gone?" she asked.

"Life was hardly worth living without you."

She laughed and smacked his arm playfully. "What *did* you do?"

"Plastered walls."

"I have a lot to tell you. I made a few sketches and I have your receipts in my satchel."

"You can clean up and rest, then tell me later."

"This evening," she said. "Come to the house for supper."

That evening Kathryn DeSmet, the schoolteacher, had been invited for supper, along with Donetta Barnes.

Irene chattered about their trip, about their dresses and the seamstress, and then launched into the tale of how they'd changed their mind about the theater once they'd seen the location.

"That was using wisdom," Sam told his oldest daughter.

Somehow it didn't seem like the right time to mention seeing Rhys there.

Later, after cleaning up, when Elisabeth and Gabe were alone in the dining room, she spread out the receipts and her drawings and proceeded to describe everything they'd purchased.

"What your father said about using wisdom," Gabe inquired. "Would some people call that common sense?"

"There is common sense, as well," she answered. "But do you remember when I said I knew inside whether something was wrong or right?" At his nod, she continued. "I knew it would be a mistake to go in there. I didn't see lightning bolts or hear an audible voice from above, but I just *knew*. In here." She touched her bodice.

He listened attentively.

"I can't say for sure something bad would have happened, but I think it might have. This way I may never know, but I probably avoided something I'd have been sorry for later—if I hadn't heeded the warning."

She showed him her drawings and described the furniture. "I'm not much of an artist. I didn't do these pieces justice."

"You bought 'most everything the house needs," he told her.

"I hope you're going to be pleased."

"You need to come out and see how the house is coming along. It's nearly finished, and you haven't seen it. I should have taken you before."

"I'd love to see it now."

"Let me know when you have a free morning, and I'll rent a rig. Or you can ride."

"I'm not much of a rider."

"Once things are more settled, you and Abigail can come for riding lessons."

She never thought she'd think it or say it, but after considering learning to ride and thinking about having Gabe as an instructor, she said, "I'd like that."

A person would've thought she'd given him the deed to a diamond mine, the way pleasure lit his features. "All right then."

The following morning, he arrived with a buggy pulled by a single black horse.

"Isn't Irene coming with us?"

"I asked her, but she had something she wanted to do."

He helped her up to the seat.

"I took the liberty of buyin' a lunch to bring along in case we get hungry."

She couldn't picture the two of them sharing a cozy picnic lunch without finding something to argue about, but she supposed it could happen. Last time they'd ridden out here they'd had Phillip along as a buffer.

Already, there was a road of sorts, where before there'd been only grass and fields. She remarked on the difference.

"All those wagons filled with supplies and all the workers coming and going have fashioned a path right to my house," he said. "Ought to make it easier on the horses when there's snow on the ground."

Up ahead, Elisabeth spotted something that surprised her and made her heart leap. In the place where they'd crossed the stream previously, a bridge had been built. Just wide enough for a wagon, but solid and well above the water.

"You built a bridge!"

"Made it easier to get the full wagons across," he told her. "And this way if Anna comes out to the ranch, it won't be as hard for her."

She turned to look at him.

"Your father mentioned that Anna was afraid of water. You didn't like crossing the stream much, either." He didn't meet her eyes. "A bridge was practical."

"Indeed."

She was grateful for the ease of crossing. *If Anna comes to the ranch,* he'd said. Interesting how he thought of her family coming to visit him. He'd probably invited Anna to come ride horses, too.

The entire clearing looked so different; the sight caught her by surprise. She'd expected a house, yes, but this was beginning to look like a ranch. A stable had been constructed, a long low building, painted white with a red roof.

A tall fellow in a faded blue shirt and a dun-colored hat was setting a fence post into the ground as they pulled up. Elisabeth didn't recognize him. Another man exited the stable and caught sight of them.

Gabe motioned him forward and called to the other, "John!"

Both men approached and removed their hats in deference to Elisabeth's company.

"This is Miss Hart. Elisabeth, this is Ward Dodd and John McEndree."

John, the one who'd been putting up the corral fence, gave her a toothy smile. "Pleasure to meet you, miss."

"These are my first two hands," Gabe told her. "They already think I'm workin' 'em hard, and the horses don't even arrive 'til next week."

John laughed. "I'll be glad when it's horses we're dealing with, and not fence posts."

The men went back to work, and Gabe ushered her toward the house. It was a long one-story home. The exterior wood siding hadn't been painted yet, but there was a door and plenty of windows.

The dooryard was dirt, of course. A walkway of

boards had been fashioned, and she supposed the wood came in handy when it rained.

The door opened into a foyer. Not as grand or as large as the Harts', but adequate. Doorways led to rooms on either side, and a hallway led back to a wood-paneled hallway on the left and a smaller hall on the right.

The smells of new wood and fresh plaster permeated the air. "I've never been inside a brand-new house before."

The first two rooms were large with floor-to-ceiling windows. "A sitting room?" she asked about the one on the left with the fireplace.

"Yep. And across the entryway is the dining room. I thought about having a cabinetmaker build storage right into this wall. What do you think?"

"It sounds perfect."

"He led her through a doorway into a small room with shelves all the way to the ceiling. "I did these myself, because they're simply functional. This area is for dishes and storing food," he explained. "And the kitchen's right through here. You can get to it this way, or by continuing on down that front hall where we came in—or of course by the back door."

The kitchen was as big as the Harts', with work spaces built along the walls and a long, waist-high table about four feet away from the stove. There was even room aside from that for a long table for eating.

"Donetta is going to love working in here," she told him. "The stove I ordered is perfect. I was concerned it might be a little big, but I see now this room called for it."

Again, there were floor-to-ceiling windows, and the view of the stables with the mountains behind was spectacular.

She remembered the diagrams he'd drawn for her and pointed. "This must be for Donetta?" None of the rooms had doors yet, so she simply walked in. The space was more than adequate, and even had a small dressing room area. "You've given her such a nice big space. And two windows. She'll like this."

"I hope so. It's going to be a big adjustment. I want to give her privacy, but don't want her to feel alone." They walked back out to the kitchen. "I'll dig a root cellar next summer."

"It looks as though you've thought of everything."

"Come on. I'll show you the rest."

"Each one of these rooms will have a small heating stove," he said. "I ordered them from a catalogue at Larken's. They should be here in another week or so."

"You'll need them when the snow and wind blow."

The hallway was wide and long with doors opening off each side. His wasn't a traditional home like those that lined the streets in Jackson Springs, but it was practical and plenty adequate for even a large family.

She supposed two and three stories atop each other saved lot space in the city. Out here he hadn't needed to concern himself with that and constructed a sprawling dwelling.

He showed her one large empty bedroom and five smaller ones. "You didn't plaster all of this yourself?"

"I'd have been here all winter," he replied. "No, I've had help throughout the entire process. I don't know how happy the people in town are now, though. They've had to find someone else to run their errands. Junie Pruitt was in the telegraph office one day when I was there and expressed an interest in coming out to see the work going on. Turns out he's pretty handy with a saw and hammer. He's been here every day since."

"Where is everyone today?"

"While the plaster's hardening this morning, we're finishing the inside of the stable, and you saw the fencing going up."

She suspected the diversion of workers may have had something to do with her visit, too.

"I'll show you where the bunkhouse is going to be."

Chapter Twenty-Two

"You already hired a couple men to work the horses with you, didn't you? Where are they staying?"

"Stables. Cook their meals over a fire for now. They're counting on that situation changing real soon." He guided her back through the house and out the front door. "As soon as the floors are varnished and there's furniture, I'll bring Donetta and Irene."

"It's really nice that there will be another woman for Irene."

"For the short time that Irene is here," he said, "yes."

Gabe helped her back into the buggy, got in and guided the horse to take them around behind the house. With this view it was plain just how long the structure was. He had chosen the level piece of ground well.

"I plan to go up in those hills and dig the largest trees I can manage," he said. "Plant several along the side of the house there. He slanted her a grin. "Can't forget to order Abigail's fruit trees, either."

"You're kind to my sisters."

"Surprised that I'm not all bad?"

"I never thought you were all bad. Or bad at all."

"When I see how they thrive in your family...how different it all seems from anything I ever knew... well, I see how I let Irene grow up without that. I don't know that I could have given it to her the same, being just a brother and only one person, but I'll never know now."

"She turned out just fine, Gabe."

He deliberately looked away, and their ride was silent for several minutes. The land sloped upward and the horse slowed. "I'm going to bring water from up there," he said. "There are springs farther up. Gravity will carry it."

"How will that work?"

"We'll build a sturdy trough, and it'll bring water right down to the house. Can even water a garden with it."

"What about in winter when it freezes?"

"In winter we'll melt snow. Are you up to walking?"

"Sure."

After finding shade for the horse, he unharnessed the animal so it could graze. He reached for her hand, and together they made their way up the hillside. They came across a deer trail, and followed the path upward. The trail reminded her of the one Josie had told her about behind their home, though this was farther from Gabe's house.

It had turned into a warm morning, and perspiration cooled her face before they reached the first spring.

Water poured from crevices in rocks and spilled into a sparkling clear pond.

"This is beautiful," she breathed.

They found a place to perch and settled to catch their breath, enjoying the peaceful sound of the water. The loamy scent of the earth and pine needles enveloped them. In the stillness, a raccoon emerged from the undergrowth and carried a twig laden with berries to the water's edge.

Elisabeth glanced at Gabe. He'd seen the animal, too. Reaching for her hand, he met her eyes. She turned her attention back just as three baby raccoons joined the first and sat on their haunches waiting for her to wash their meal.

She drank from the stream, and the babies followed her example. Minutes later, she turned and nature's parade disappeared back into the foliage.

"If a person sat here long enough, he'd see deer and all manner of creatures," Gabe said. "The entire area is covered with tracks."

"What about something dangerous, like a mountain lion?" she asked.

"Wouldn't do to come up here without a gun," he advised.

Her gaze slid to his vest, where the bump of his holster was visible.

At the water's edge, they cupped their hands and drank the cold clear water until they'd had their fill.

Gabe wiped his chin with the back of his hand and studied her in the sunlight. The sparkling reflection from the water cast darts of light across her face and hair. Maybe it was this place or maybe it was because she'd softened toward him however minutely, but she seemed more at ease. Her whole demeanor was less rigid, and her enjoyment genuine.

Knowing he didn't stand a chance with her didn't prevent him from imagining how it would be if she married him and this became their home.

He didn't even want to admit the fact to himself, but during his hours of work, whether it was sawing and planing logs or pounding shingles on the roof, he pictured her living here. He imagined the two of them sitting in front of the fireplace. He imagined sharing a room and a bed. He imagined children.

She'd run for the hills if she had an inkling of his thoughts. But the seeds were planted in his mind's eye and he watered them daily.

Her family could come for Sunday dinners. Irene and Gil would join them. Their children and Irene's children would grow up part of a family.

His throat got tight at the wistful thought. He reached for her hand. "Come on."

He harnessed the horse and they took the buggy even farther from the ranch house, exploring the sights and enjoying the day. "There's another deer trail," she said, spotting one heading into the brush on a hillside.

"Want to follow it?" he asked.

"Let's."

"I'm getting hungry. I'll grab the food this time." He took the small crate from the rear of the buggy.

The trail led them higher and deeper into the woods

than before. "Will we find our way back out?" she asked.

"We head downhill, right?"

"We should have left breadcrumbs."

"What good would that do? The birds would eat them."

She'd been leading, and she turned to look back at him. "I was kidding. That's what Hansel and Gretel did."

"Who are they?"

"It's a children's fairy tale."

"Oh."

Here the smell of the forest changed. The verdant scent of pine needles was masked by a sulfurous smell. The air seemed more humid, and Gabe broke out in a sweat.

It wasn't long before the trail leveled out and brought them to a long steaming pool. At first he thought the vapor was a phenomenon caused by warm air and cold water, but the humidity and the smell said otherwise. There was no sound of running water here. The water seemed to move with an inner life.

Gabe set down the crate and walked straight to the rocks lining the pool, where he knelt and plunged his hand into the water. Even though he'd expected the temperature, the warmth shocked him. He plunged in his other hand. "It's *hot*."

Elisabeth drew up beside him and knelt, the hem of her skirt falling into the water. She dabbled her fingers and then her hand, and her eyes widened. She raised a questioning gaze up to him.

"A mineral spring," he said in amazement.

"I've read about them," she said. "Some think they have restorative healing abilities."

He nodded.

"There are places you can go to bathe in mineral springs. Wealthy people do it."

He nodded again. "And pay a lot of money for the privilege." His mind rolled back over the incidents he'd questioned at the time, but dismissed. "This could be why Rhys Jackson keeps offering me twice what my land is worth—or what I thought it was worth."

"Do you think he knows this is here?"

"There's probably more than one spot where the water seeps," he said. "It's being fed from underground. Probably bubbling up wherever it finds an exit."

"Do you suppose he's known about this for a long time?"

"And kept it under his hat. He said he'd looked for the property owner, and now we know why. He wanted to buy the land and make himself rich."

"*You* could be rich, Gabe."

"It's a tempting thought after all I've spent on building my ranch." He took off his hat and ran his wet hands through his hair. "I don't know that I'd want a lot of people traipsing across my land to get here though."

"You can think about it," she suggested.

"I don't know that I want to eat here," he said. "It's warm."

"I'm getting rather used to it," she said. "And I'm hungry."

He agreed and unpacked the food.

Elisabeth unwrapped a turkey sandwich. "This is a treat."

"I wasn't sure what you like or don't like."

"I like everything." She paused before taking a bite. "Except olives."

"Half the crate is olives," he teased. "Guess I'll have to eat them myself.

"Guess you will."

After they'd finished their sandwiches, he washed shiny red apples. To finish off the meal, he uncovered slices of cake, which they had to eat with their fingers because there were no forks.

She laughed and washed her hands in the warm water. "Cleanup's not a problem, but we can't drink this."

With a flourish, he produced a single jar of buttermilk and no cups, so they took turns drinking from the jar.

"I still want some water," she said, once they'd finished.

"I'll find you some cold water," he promised.

"I haven't been on a picnic for a long time. Of course we ate out of doors on Independence Day, but other than that."

"I ate half my meals over a campfire when I was on the trail," he said. "Ate a lot of hardtack and biscuits. Shot an occasional rabbit or squirrel. Nothing too big to eat in one sitting."

"We ate a lot of rabbits on our way west," she said. "I don't remember having squirrel."

"It's not prairie game." He gazed across the water,

again envisioning a family. "Do you think your sisters would like to swim here?"

"I think they would. It's not frightening in any way. In fact it's rather like a big washtub. We'll have to buy bathing wear first. We have none."

"If it involves shopping, Irene will join you." He chuckled.

They moved to sit comfortably on a bank of grass and pine needles. "You speak differently when you talk about Irene today," she said.

He nodded and took the stone from his pocket. "I can't change the past. That's what you told me."

"I also said you'd done the very best you could for her."

"How many stones are in *your* pocket today?"

She reached into her skirt and produced three on her open palm.

"What is it they symbolize?"

"Sacrifice. Dedication."

"Seems like I remember you said they remind you of the choices you've made and the results of those choices."

She looked away. "Yes. That, too."

"Which is it?"

She glanced back at him. "What do you mean?"

"Well, I've thought a lot since you gave mine to me. I stopped blaming myself for things I couldn't change. I regret missing those years with my sister, but I can't change it. You helped me look at my plans for Irene honestly. I can only move forward and be glad for her because she's in love and very happy."

"That's good, Gabe."

"I'm having trouble with the logic of the stone, however."

"Why's that?"

"Because when I hold it every day, it reminds me of the past, not the future."

Elisabeth studied his hand, now loosely holding the rock and opened her palm to look at her collection.

"You said we can't change the past or the poor decisions we've made," he said.

"That's right."

"But you carry around those rocks that remind you of something you feel guilty about. I was reading in Philippians…"

Her head shot up and she raised her eyebrows.

"Can't remember all those words like you can, but the gist of it was that Paul said we should forget those things that are behind us and just look toward the goal out in front."

Elisabeth knew exactly which scripture he referred to. She could have quoted it perfectly. *I count not myself to have apprehended: but this one thing I do, forgetting those things which are behind, and reaching forth unto those things which are before…*

Before her sat a man who'd never read a Bible until he'd met their family. Now he spoke about truths of God's Word. He hadn't quoted scripture the way she could, but he'd obviously interpreted the verses and understood their meaning in a way she never had.

At first she wanted to be angry with him for questioning her thinking or for believing he had a better understanding than she…but she really wanted to get mad because he'd forced her to think about something she'd clung to for a long time.

The stones did remind her of sacrifice. And choices. And her mother.

Her eyes smarted and her nostrils stung. But the memories the symbols provoked were not happy memories of her childhood or of her mother as a sweet-natured, pretty blonde woman. They were memories of a woman floating facedown in the water, fair hair snagged in the brush along the shore. The reminders evoked memories of an ashen-faced person being wrapped in her parents' wedding quilt and lowered into a grave.

All the memories made her regret her fear and behavior that fateful day. The mementos reminded her she couldn't go back and fix what had happened. And when she thought about her regrets logically, she believed just as Gabe had said weeks ago that she'd been a frightened girl and had done what anyone else would have done in the same situation. She'd had no way of knowing that she would have been saved—or even that her mother could have been rescued in time.

She couldn't live those hours over to change the outcome, but she relived what she perceived as her mistake every time she looked at or touched one of these stones.

The stones were her past. She didn't know what her future held, but she couldn't let it be filled with regret. From here on out changes had to be made.

Elisabeth got to her feet. One at a time, she threw the rocks into the steaming pond. Each stone made a satisfying plunk and created circles on the surface before the water swallowed it into its depths.

"What have you done?" Gabe now stood beside her.

"I put the past behind me." She stared at the water.

Another rock sailed through the air and landed with a watery plunk where hers had disappeared. She turned to find Gabe staring at the spot where he'd thrown his stone. "Hope that was okay," he said. "It bein' a gift and all."

"It was perfectly okay. I'll give you another gift to replace it."

"Not necessary."

"I know. Thank you, Gabe."

"For what?"

"For opening my eyes to the fact that I was punishing myself."

"Wasn't me," he said. "That Paul fella said it."

She laughed then, a laugh that came from deep in her belly and echoed across the water and off the rocks. She laughed until she wore herself out and had to stop to breathe.

Gabe shook his head. "As long as you're laughing, I have something else to say that you might find amusing."

She composed herself in preparation. "I'm ready."

For a moment she thought he'd changed his mind about sharing whatever it was he wanted to say, but then he pursed his lips and took a deep breath. "I don't expect you to do anything with this. I don't expect anything. I just want to say it, and then I'll have it off my chest."

"Oh, my goodness. Is this something serious and not funny at all?"

"I guess that depends how you look at it."

"All right. What is it?"

"It won't change anything. You're still you and I'm still me."

"Gabe," she said impatiently.

"I just want to be honest."

This time she sighed. "Now you're starting to scare me because you won't just come out with—"

"I love you."

Chapter Twenty-Three

His words stopped the sentence she'd been forming—and her brain—for about thirty seconds. Had she heard correctly?

"I realize I can't measure up to the standards you've set for your future husband. I'm not going to regret that fact or bemoan it, because I can't change who I am. I can't change that I wasn't raised in a family like yours or that I never really knew about Jesus until you spoke of Him. Until your father taught me. Now I'm inspired to be a better man. And that's the future.

"I've lived a life you can't condone, and that's just a fact. So that's why I'm sayin' you don't have to do anything with the information. You don't even have to respond. It's okay. I just wanted to say it. Just once."

He turned and picked up the crate.

It took her a moment to get herself oriented and follow him. He led the way down the hillside, and the whole time she thought over his pronouncement. She was thankful he hadn't expected her to say anything, because she didn't know what she would have said. She felt as though she was a pebble rolling down a hill to spin off a cliff into midair. Her rational thoughts were suspended while she processed Gabe's startling proclamation.

They arrived at the buggy and Gabe guided the horse back to the house. He dipped water from a barrel with a dented tin cup and handed it to her. The liquid was warm and nothing like the cold-water spring they'd visited, but it was wet and she thanked him.

"Well, you've seen it all," he told her.

She took a last look at the house. "You've done an amazing job."

"The first horses will be here in a couple of weeks."

"Were you serious about bringing my family here? To the mineral springs?"

"Yes, of course."

She nodded. "Good. When I return, I'm going to bring the rest of the stones and throw them in."

"How many more are there?"

"Maybe twenty or so."

"You're welcome here anytime. Not just with an invite or with your family."

She blushed, unable to prevent the rush of embarrassment. The last thing she wanted was for their friendship to get uncomfortable.

As though her high color had signaled him, he said, "I don't want things to get awkward between us, Elisabeth. We'd just settled into something manageable."

"I don't want that, either."

"All right. We're friends?"

"Yes. Friends."

He helped her aboard the buggy one last time and headed toward Jackson Springs.

Midafternoon, Gabe left Elisabeth in the shade on the boardwalk and pushed open the door on which gold letters spelled out the name of the bank above the name of the man he'd come to see.

The teller recognized him, and the man greeted him warmly. "What transaction can we help you with today, Mr. Taggart?"

"I've come to see Mr. Jackson."

"He's in his office." The man turned as though to exit the caged area. "I'll let him know you're here."

"No need," Gabe interrupted. "The one with the big bold letters that spell his name, right?"

"Mr. Jackson doesn't like to be interrupted without an appointment, sir."

Gabe strode past the lobby and down a short hallway, where he opened the office door without a pause.

Startled, Rhys looked up from a ledger on his desk. "Mr. Taggart?"

He stood and reached behind him for his jacket.

"Don't bother to dress for me," Gabe said.

It was obvious the man was uncomfortable at not having had time to prepare for a visit or don his jacket. He gestured for Gabe to take one of the plush chairs that faced his desk. "Please have a seat."

"This won't take long."

"What can I help you with today?"

"It's about my land."

His expression lightened, and his eyebrows rose. "Have you had a change of heart about selling?"

"It's funny you should ask."

With an eager step, Rhys came around the corner of the desk. "I'm prepared to sign a cashier's check over to you."

"No need to pay."

Rhys stopped in his tracks. "What?"

"What are friends for, right? I just came to tell you to let your mother know she might want to buy a bathing costume."

"What?"

"I recall her saying she has a touch of lumbago. Perhaps a nice hot mineral bath will relieve those symptoms for a spell. Bring her out, why don't you?"

Rhys's face turned as red as a ripe tomato. It was warm in the room, but Gabe detected his color had nothing to do with the temperature, but rather the anger and embarrassment of his deceit being discovered. He stiffened, straightened his tie unnecessarily and walked back to his chair where he dropped before mopping his face with a handkerchief. "A mineral bath, you say?"

"Yes. Who'd have known there were hot springs bubbling from those rocks up there? Isn't that a wonder?"

"Yes, indeed." Rhys folded the handkerchief. "Should you change your mind, I might be able to facilitate a sale. There are rumors that former President Grant is looking for a vacation spot."

"What a coincidence." Gabe flattened a palm on the desk and leaned forward. "I won't be selling. Not to you, not to the former president, not to the king of England should he come lookin'." Gabe straightened. "What do you say we never talk about this again?"

Rhys's expression eased a measure. "Not to anyone else, either?"

"I won't say a word. Miss Hart will likely tell her father, however."

Rhys sighed and dabbed his face again.

"But it'll blow over. We all make mistakes, don't we? I couldn't let this go, you understand that, without letting you know I was aware of what you did. Now we're all wiser." He headed for the door. "And I hope smarter."

Rhys gave a sheepish nod and Gabe exited the room.

Ten minutes later, Elisabeth knocked on the open door to her father's office.

Sam looked up and spotted them both. "How was your ride?"

"Gabe's house is almost finished. It's going to be an excellent home."

"We learned something today," Gabe added. He went on to explain how Rhys had been making offers on his land and then explained how they'd discovered the mineral springs.

"I don't want to think he was doing something underhanded," Sam said. "But it sounds as though he knew all along, doesn't it?"

"There's something I haven't mentioned to either of you," Elisabeth brought up. "The time didn't seem right until now."

"What is it, daughter?" Sam asked.

"When Irene and I took the carriage to the theater in Denver and learned it was above a gaming hall, we saw Rhys with a group of men. He went inside that place."

Sam shook his head. "That surprises me."

Gabe didn't appear to share his feelings.

"I take it you're not surprised?" Sam asked.

"In my experience, most people don't have the same...*convictions* your family does. Rhys strikes me as a greedy fellow."

"Since he comes to my church, I suppose I'll have to talk to him."

"Before we came here, I let him know I was on to him."

"His mother probably isn't aware of his behavior, and there's no need to draw her into it," Sam said.

"It was okay that I told you?" Elisabeth said.

"Yes, of course," Sam answered. "Just because something's uncomfortable doesn't mean we don't need to address it and handle it. Now finish telling me your reactions to Gabe's ranch."

"There aren't any horses or cows yet."

Sam and Gabe chuckled and Elisabeth finished her descriptions.

That night Elisabeth went to her room shortly after supper and read her Bible. Finding the verses Gabe had called to her attention, she read the chapter in Philippians. Those words had never been as real to her as they became at that moment. It had taken a man who'd only seen those verses for the first time and spoken about them to bring them to life.

Glancing around, she got up and gathered the individual piles of stones and placed them inside a drawstring bag. No longer was she going to look at the symbols every day and regret a past that had been out of her control. She set the bag in her armoire to await her next trip to the mineral springs.

After she'd turned down the wick and plunged the room into darkness, she got comfortable on her bed and closed her eyes. Words and images swirled in her head like colors in a kaleidoscope.

What was she supposed to do with the news Gabe had delivered that day? He'd told her he wasn't expecting an answer or anything in return. He'd just wanted to say the words. But she had to lock her mind around them some way.

He loved her?

I just wanted to say it. Just once. Those words told her he wasn't going to bring it up again.

But the knowledge was there. Like a heart beating beneath a breast. He loved her. He loved her. He loved her.

She and Gil had been friends a long time, and while they did share a friendly affection, neither had ever had the inclination to express love. Yes, God's children are commanded to love one another, but this love was something else entirely.

How was she supposed to sleep?

I've lived a life you can't condone.

I can't measure up to the standards you've set.

He'd been taking sole responsibility for her inability to accept him.

I can't change who I am. I can't change that I wasn't raised in a family like yours or that I never really knew about Jesus until you spoke of Him…until your father taught me.

But he was changing who he was. At that point, she'd been too stunned to say that. Too stunned to say anything.

I'm inspired to be a better man. That's the future.

She'd seen changes in him since his arrival. She believed his inspiration wasn't created by anything she'd said or done, but fueled by the examples he was reading about in the Bible.

He'd gone to great lengths to provide for and educate his sister. He'd wanted to make a home for her… and he wanted her to have a good husband. More importantly, he'd been willing to forfeit some of his plans for them because he wanted her to be happy. Irene may have complained a bit about his overprotectiveness at the beginning, but Elisabeth suspected she truly appreciated his concern.

If she was really honest with herself, Elisabeth had to admit she'd been a little jealous of how easily he made friends and how quickly he'd acclimated himself into a new community. People liked him and some even admired him.

As though glossing over his ability to make friends, he'd said he was good at reading people. Understanding people was a gift, however, and he had the gift.

He'd undeniably saved Donetta Barnes's life. That had been an amazing feat of skill and bravery, but the thing that stuck out the most to Elisabeth was the fact that he'd consequently found ways to take care of her now that she was widowed.

The congregation had taken her food, but Gabe had given her a job. That was an act of mercy and kindness, but also one conceived in wisdom.

He wasn't the person she'd first thought. He wasn't callused or heartless. Just the opposite in fact.

And she enjoyed kissing him.

How was she supposed to sleep now?

The following week, sooner than expected, Gabe moved Irene and Donetta out to the ranch house. He gathered them and Elisabeth instructed them how to manage a horse and buggy.

"Once you know this you won't have to rely on me or one of the hands to get you back and forth from town. And you're going to need to learn one more thing."

He led them behind the house where hay bales had been stacked and bottles set atop them. He presented each of them with a rifle.

Irene accepted hers. "You're going to show us how to shoot these?"

"Yep. Never know when a coyote or mountain lion or even a two-legged critter will turn mean."

Elisabeth wanted to protect herself, but she didn't believe she could shoot another person. "Will you show us how to aim for a place that won't kill a human?"

"Yes, I will, Elisabeth."

He first taught them how to load the chamber and how to keep the barrel lowered for safety. Eventually the lessons progressed to target practice.

Donetta had experience, so right away she was the best shot. Irene jerked and jumped back each time she fired, so she didn't hit much. But Elisabeth was as precise and efficient about aiming and shooting as she was about everything. Within an hour, the bottles she aimed for shattered nearly every shot.

"I might have known you'd be my prize pupil," Gabe said to her later. "The one who hates guns."

"If I'm going to learn, I'm going to learn to do it well," she replied.

That week and the next were filled with normal activities in addition to shooting practice and Irene's wedding plans. Elisabeth stayed busier than ever.

Irene invited her for dinner one evening, and they sat at the long table in the new kitchen. "How do you like that stove?" she asked Donetta.

"It's a dream," the older woman replied.

Gabe entered the back door. "I saw the buggy and knew it was you. Is your rifle under the seat?"

"Irene invited me. And yes, it is."

"Told you you're welcome anytime even without an invitation." His hair was damp and his tanned face ruddy as though he'd recently washed. "The hands take their meals with us."

"I remember."

As Irene helped set the last few bowls on the table, John and Ward entered and hung their hats on pegs.

"How do, Mizz Hart," Ward said and John, too, greeted her, giving her a broad smile that showed all his teeth. Both of them were freshly scrubbed and wearing clean shirts. They seated themselves across from each other in about the middle of the table.

Gabe held out Mrs. Barnes's chair before taking a seat at the head. Everyone quieted, with heads lowered.

"Thank You for this food, Lord," Gabe said.

Elisabeth was so surprised she looked at him from the corner of her eye.

"Thank You that we have plenty of work to keep us busy. Keep us safe and well. In Jesus's name, amen."

The prayer hadn't been particularly eloquent or lengthy, but the fact that he'd said a prayer at all threw her thoughts askew.

Donetta picked up a heaping bowl of mashed potatoes and handed it to John. The food was simple fare of sliced roast, potatoes and carrots, but there was plenty of it and the men ate more than Elisabeth had ever seen anyone pile on their plate. They worked long, strenuous hours out of doors, and obviously worked up an appetite.

Irene met her eyes and grinned, obviously not a newcomer to this dinner table. "We pick up our dresses in Denver day after tomorrow."

"After supper show Elisabeth the beds and rugs and bureaus," Gabe said. "So she can see what her choices look like in the house."

After they'd finished the meal and eaten rice pudding, they drank hot cups of dark sweetened coffee. Donetta stacked dishes. Elisabeth carried bowls to the sink and the woman took them from her. "Not here, you don't. This is my job. You run along with your friend."

Irene showed her all the pieces of furniture they'd shopped for, and Elisabeth was pleased with how they looked in the rooms.

Irene excused herself for a few minutes, and Elisabeth stepped out the back door. She appreciated that Gabe had built a covered porch on the back of the house, and she stood in the shade of the roof, gazing toward the hillsides with their variegated shades of green.

Gabe spotted her and strode over. He didn't climb the stairs, but stood below her. "While you're in Denver, take Irene to a few of those furniture makers and see what she likes best. If you can somehow manage it without her knowing, I'd like it if you ordered a bedroom set or maybe a dining table or whatever takes her fancy."

"Without her knowledge?"

He nodded. "As a wedding gift. They're going to have that house and will need things to fill it. I don't figure Gil can buy it all on his lawman's wages."

She wanted to run down the stairs and hug him. Kiss him maybe. His thoughtful gesture touched her. "I already have somewhat of an idea what she likes from our previous trip, but I'll ask questions." She studied him in the fading daylight. "If I had an older brother, I couldn't ask for a better one than you."

He returned her perusal, letting his gaze take in her hair and fall on her dress. "I don't think of you as a sister, Elisabeth."

"I know."

The sound of hoofbeats reached them, and Gabe's

attention shifted. Gil galloped toward them, then reined the horse to a walk and stopped several feet from the porch.

"Evenin', Deputy. Is Irene expecting you?"

Gil climbed down and used his hat to swat dust from his pant legs. "No. I thought I'd be working this evening, but Dan was feeling better and took his own shift back." He glanced up. "What kind of trouble are you finding here, Lis?"

"I'm well, thanks."

He grinned. "You're always well." He turned back to Gabe. "Is she inside?"

"She'll be out in a minute," Elisabeth replied.

"Have a seat on the porch there," Gabe said. "Elisabeth and I are taking a walk. Join me?"

She gathered her skirts and descended the steps.

A long low building had been framed with a stone fireplace at one end. The structure was a new addition since her last visit. "The bunkhouse?" she guessed.

"The men are lookin' forward to moving from the stable," he said. "I talked with a rancher who runs a spread up by Pagosa Springs. He told me he'd placed sod in between two layers of wood on the roof. Before the shingles went on his bunkhouse and barn. Holds in the heat, he says. I'm gonna try it."

Elisabeth considered how their relationship had evolved from that first day on the train until this moment as he spoke to her about the development of his ranch and day-to-day happenings.

She trusted God for her provision and her safety, and in doing so she had to believe He'd had a hand in how they'd met. "Have you ever thought," she asked, "that you and I could have taken different trains? But we were aboard the same one."

"That's a fact."

"Those bandits could have held up a different train and hurt innocent people, but they chose the train the two of us were on."

"I've thought a lot about people and the choices they make. The choices we all make. Remember the day Doc Barnes was killed?"

"Clearly."

"I asked you how God could have let that happen."

"I remember."

"You told me God has given each of us free will to make choices."

"That's right."

"If I believe that—and I do now—then God didn't put those bandits on that train. They had free will to do as they chose. They chose to do wrong. Ours was the train they picked." Their walk took them to the stream that ran behind the clearing where the house and outbuildings sat. It was a narrow rivulet of water, only about five feet wide, but flourishing trees grew along the banks. "You and I have free will, too. How can God use us?"

"Because we listen to that still small voice on the inside," she reminded him. "God doesn't have to manipulate us. He simply speaks to us, and we respond." She studied the branches of a huge oak tree that towered over them. "I've never told you this. I was planning to stay in Morning Creek another day, but when I woke up that morning, I felt very strongly that I should go home. I packed my bag and bought my ticket."

Gabe bent to pick up a stick. "I read in the Psalms that God knows everything about us. He knew us before we were born. He knew you'd take that particular train."

"Nothing is a surprise to God. He wasn't up in heaven wringing His hands when He saw those robbers get on board. I'm sure it breaks His heart when people do sinful things, but He made a plan to rescue innocent people by sending you."

"You're saying God worked through me?"

"You were willing. That's all He needs. You're important to Him. He had a plan for you, too, just as He created a plan for all mankind by sending Jesus."

"It took me a while to grasp that when Sam told me, but I understand how big God's love is now. I've accepted His love for me."

Elisabeth got a lump in her throat. She walked several feet away and stood looking out over the water. The sight and sound no longer had the hold over her it once had. She had released her guilt and her grief. Gabe had helped her do that. One more reason she knew God's hand was at work in bringing him here.

Tears welled in her eyes and blurred the sparkling stream in her vision. Why this man, Lord? Why not the man she had believed for—the one just like her father?

She composed herself and turned. He squatted a few feet from the edge of the water, breaking a stick into pieces and tossing bits in. He'd left his hat back at the house, and she studied the way his dark hair curled over his collar and around his ears. A lock fell forward over his forehead.

He was pleasing to look upon, no doubt about that. And he was smart and enterprising, with a plan for a ranch and the tenacity and grit to make it happen.

Her father had taken their family west because he had a vision of a new life, and he'd faced adversities to make it happen—continuing on even after the death of his beloved wife. He'd loved his daughters enough to marry a woman he wasn't sure he could love, but who would be there for them.

Gabe loved his sister like that. Enough to sacrifice and do what he'd believed was best for her.

Her father loved God with all his heart and served Him in all his ways. He taught people about God's love by example and through his preaching.

Elisabeth thought of that simple prayer Gabe had spoken at the supper table. He had once said he couldn't change who he was, but he had been changing ever since Elisabeth had met him. *I can't change that I wasn't raised in a family like yours or that I never really knew about Jesus until you spoke of Him. Until your father taught me. Now I'm inspired to be a better man. And that's the future.*

Her father had been raised in a Christian home, taught of the Lord his entire life, so of course he had more experience and eloquence. But maybe the important thing was what a person did with the knowledge they had. Gabe's hired hands saw the example of a man who sat down to pray at the supper table. Maybe he was their only link to hear about God's love for them.

Sam Hart loved people and went out of his way to help them. Gabe had provided a job—a good job and a home—for a widow. How could a person show more compassion than that?

It had been easy to set a lofty expectation, knowing there wasn't another man like her father and thereby conveniently keeping herself out of the marriage market.

She'd been so afraid of losing herself that she hadn't been open to love. She'd envied Irene's ability to make herself vulnerable. Love made a person transparent, and for a long time Elisabeth hadn't wanted anyone seeing through her.

No, there wasn't another Sam Hart.

But there was only one Gabe Taggart, as well.

And she loved him.

Chapter Twenty-Four

The sun had dropped low in the sky, casting her long shadow across the grass as she walked toward him. At her approach he threw the stick in the water and turned to sit on the bank and face her. One side of his mouth turned up in the teasing grin that had once provoked her, but now turned her insides to jelly.

"I recognize that determined look." He reached for her hand. "Come sit beside me. Should I be scared?"

She took his hand, but instead of sitting on the ground, she plopped herself into his lap so hard, he released a surprised, "Ooof."

"I'm sorry. Did I hurt your ribs?"

"What are you doing?" He steadied her with one hand on her elbow.

"Putting an end to a big mistake."

"What do you mean?"

"I'm pigheaded and a perfectionist. I like things orderly."

"Is there a surprise coming?"

"And I'm a coward."

"Not that I ever noticed."

She placed her hands on his shoulders. "You changed your whole life, Gabe. You moved right into a town where you'd never lived before and you made friends. You embraced something completely foreign to you—the concept of God's love and His will for your life. You move forward and you don't look back. You abandoned your past for a fresh start."

"How does that make you a coward?"

"It doesn't. I was making a comparison."

"To you? You don't have a past to bury."

"I did. I hung on to those stones so I could nurse my guilt. You opened my eyes to that. I held everyone at arm's length by expecting so much of them that they could never live up to my model of perfection.

"But I wasn't perfect. Far from it. I was afraid. Afraid of loving…of being loved…afraid I'd let someone down or that I'd be let down. Afraid of so many things. That's how I've been cowardly."

"I believe you're a brave woman who stands up for what she believes and for the people she loves."

"I wanted a husband just like my father."

"There's nothing wrong with that standard, Elisabeth."

"Except that there isn't another man like him. And if there was, I wouldn't want him."

"Why not?"

"Because I already love a man."

His expression flickered with uncertainty. Overhead the leaves of the oak tree rustled in the breeze. Crickets chirped in the underbrush. "You do?"

"I've fallen for a man who's generous and compassionate and brave. He shares my faith, and he has a good plan for the future. A future I want to be part of."

"Elisabeth, if there's a surprise coming, out with it. If you tell me this man is Junie Pruitt or Lester Quinn, I'm going to dump you right out of my lap into that water."

"It's not Junie Pruitt or Lester Quinn." She placed a hand on either side of his face and brushed her palms over the warm rough texture of his lean cheeks.

He brought his hands up her back to hold her more closely and stared into her eyes.

"This man has already said he loves me. And I'm praying he means it."

He threaded the fingers of one hand into her hair. "He means it with all his heart."

"He told me he would only say it once, so I can't be sure."

"That was before he thought there was a hope of having his love returned."

"And now?" Her breath caught in her throat as she waited.

"I love you, Elisabeth. I've been in love with you since the moment you looked me in the eye and challenged me to get out my gun and do something about those train robbers."

Her heart was already pounding, but at his words it raced harder. "I *what?*"

"I was content to sit there minding my own business, let them take their watches and baubles and be gone.

You on the other hand, insisted you'd seen my gun and challenged me to stop them."

"I did no such thing."

"You did."

She thought back over those moments, fraught with tension and fear. She'd done precisely as he'd said. "I did."

They looked into each other's eyes. He grinned.

She leaned forward and kissed him, and he met her eagerly. She put every apology, every regret, every hope into that kiss, then leaned back, still framing his head in her hands. "I love you."

"Enough to marry me?"

Her eyes stung. "Enough to marry you tomorrow."

He kissed her soundly. "We'd better wait until after Gil and Irene are married or we'll steal their thunder."

"But no longer than that," she insisted.

"No longer than that."

Epilogue

On a sunny morning mid-September Gabe stood beside Samuel Hart at the front of the church. Constance Graham played the wedding march and the notes from the old organ made his heart skip a beat.

The front pews were filled with family—and people who would soon be family after this ceremony. His sister held baby Rachel, who slept soundly. Her new husband, Gil, stood beside her, his expression soft as he looked down at his new wife.

Clasping hands, Abigail and Anna, dressed in frilly pale blue dresses, gave him broad and encouraging smiles. They turned every few seconds to peer over heads to the back of the church in anticipation of their sister's entrance.

Josie gave Gabe a nod and a smile. The service hadn't even started yet, and she took a white hankie from her sleeve and dabbed the corners of her eyes. Beside her were John and Peter, and directly behind them stood Kalli with Phillip.

The doors opened and she stood haloed in sunlight,

a vision in white satin and layers of lace and pearls. She'd spent numerous hours on the details of the dress and the veil, but all he saw was Elisabeth. The woman he wanted as his wife from this day forward.

Instead of a practical braid, her blond hair had been fashioned into loops fastened to the back of her head, while long curls hung down her back. The veil wasn't long or cumbersome, but a small stylish embellishment that barely covered her eyes.

Since Sam was the father of the bride as well as the preacher, he waited until she'd come halfway forward and then went to accompany her the rest of the way. He folded the veil back from her eyes and gazed into them, then took her hand and kissed her fingers.

He then turned to Gabe and offered Elisabeth's hand. With emotion thick in his voice, he said, "I give my daughter to you to marry."

Gabe accepted her hand. When her shining blue eyes turned to him, his heart stopped altogether. For those moments no one else existed. She was the most beautiful woman he'd ever set eyes upon. And she was looking at him with such love, she took his breath away.

His heart started beating again. He took a breath. *Thank You, Lord, for giving me this woman and a whole new beginning.*

"We are gathered here in front of these witnesses, and in the name of our Lord God..."

Gabe Taggart was marrying the preacher's daughter.

* * * * *

Dear Reader,

I heard from many readers who enjoyed *The Preacher's Wife* and were eager for more stories about the Hart family, so it's my pleasure to bring you Elisabeth and Gabe. Elisabeth expends a lot of energy on perfectionism and organization. I wholeheartedly relate to her character. It's hard for Elisabeth to let go of the way things *should be done* and simply enjoy that a task is accomplished. Anything disorganized or unplanned makes her feel out of control. A train holdup and a handsome rescuer are definitely not in her plans. Shaking up her world was fun!

Thanks to all of you who take time from your busy lives to write and let me know you've enjoyed my stories. I appreciate each letter and email. I pray you're having a wonderful summer and enjoying your many blessings!

Visit my blog for drawings and book news: *http://cherylstjohn.blogspot.com.*

All my best,

Cheryl St. John

:)

QUESTIONS FOR DISCUSSION

1. Because she lost her mother in such a terrible manner, Elisabeth's need for control ran deep. We often hear the adage, "Let go and let God," but releasing control isn't as easy as it sounds. We've all probably been in a situation where it took us longer than it should have to release a problem. Are there any particular scriptures that help you remember God wants to take your burdens?

2. Gabe hid the fact that he was a bounty hunter from his sister and kept it a secret in his new community. Everyone has things in their past that they'd rather not have revealed. What does Micah 7:19 have to say about our past transgressions?

3. Gabe treated Elisabeth differently than everyone else, therefore her family members and the town had a glowing opinion of him. Their praise and approval irritated her. How should we react when we are the undeserving target of someone's animosity?

4. Elisabeth surprised Gabe by taking his hand and praying aloud for a neighbor. She learned from her father to speak to God as openly as she would to anyone with whom she had a relationship. Which character do you relate to: Gabe, being uncomfort-

able about the prayer? Or Elisabeth, doing what comes naturally?

5. Gabe enjoyed baiting Elisabeth, and she was never sure if his questions about the Bible were posed simply to rile her or because he really wanted to know. Why do you think he had so much fun provoking her?

6. Elisabeth had physical reactions to the memories of losing her mother, specifically to the sound of rushing water. Do you think reactions like that are out of our control or do you believe we have authority over our bodies and our reactions?

7. When Elisabeth's young brother Phillip mentioned her mother was in heaven, Gabe said he thought people made up their own beliefs to get them through grief or to justify their behavior. Why do you think that statement was so shocking to Elisabeth? Do you know someone who dismisses your beliefs in a similar manner? How can you best make your reaction to another's unbelief into a good example?

8. Gabe was constantly being recognized as the man who shot the train robbers. He really didn't want to be known for that single act, but it was the first thing people thought of. If there was one thing that people remembered about you and talked about, what would you want it to be?

9. Gabe's sister, Irene, told him she had prayed for his safety all the years they were apart. Was there someone who prayed for you before you knew how to believe God on your own? Can you think of a time you know God protected you from harm because of a previous prayer?

10. When Dr. Barnes and his wife were held hostage by outlaws, Gabe and Sam had level heads, while Irene went into near-hysterics. If initial reactions to a critical situation show a person's faith level, how do you think Elisabeth's behavior measured up?

11. When Elisabeth and Irene discovered the opera house was located above a gambling establishment, Elisabeth knew in her spirit that it wouldn't be wise to enter. She had a difficult time explaining that to Gabe. How would you tell someone who didn't share your faith that you'd had a warning from God?

12. Gabe's character growth during the story evolved because of his exposure to the faith of the Harts and his sister, and finally because he took it upon himself to read the Bible. Elisabeth thought Gabe might be the only example his hired men ever saw of a man who prayed. You may be the only Jesus that a friend or coworker has ever seen. Are there any changes you want to make now, so that the light of His love shines through you?

INSPIRATIONAL

Inspirational romances to warm your heart & soul.

HISTORICAL

TITLES AVAILABLE NEXT MONTH

Available July 12, 2011

CALICO BRIDE
Buttons and Bobbins
Jillian Hart

FRONTIER FATHER
Dorothy Clark

SECOND CHANCE FAMILY
Winnie Griggs

HEARTS IN FLIGHT
Patty Smith Hall

REQUEST YOUR FREE BOOKS!

2 FREE INSPIRATIONAL NOVELS
PLUS 2
FREE
MYSTERY GIFTS

Love Inspired
HISTORICAL
INSPIRATIONAL HISTORICAL ROMANCE

Love Inspired

After losing his wife and son, Adrian Lapp has vowed never to marry again. But widow Faith Martin—the newest resident of the Amish community of Hope Springs—captivates him from their first meeting. Can Adrian open his heart to the possibility of love again?

The Farmer Next Door
by Patricia Davids

BRIDES OF
Amish Country

*Available in July
wherever books are sold.*

www.LoveInspiredBooks.com

LI87679

![Love Inspired HISTORICAL]

Bestselling author

JILLIAN HART

brings readers another
heartwarming story from

Safe, predictable Angel Falls, Montana, is Lila Lawson's
home—but she secretly wishes it had adventures like the
novels she loves to read. Then new deputy Burke Hannigan
stumbles into her father's mercantile, gravely injured, and
Lila gets more excitement than she can handle!

Look for

Calico Bride

Available in July
wherever books are sold.

www.LoveInspiredBooks.com

LIH82875